DISCORDIA

THE ELEVENTH DIMENSION

DISCORDIA

THE ELEVENTH DIMENSION

DENA K. SALMON

Disney · HYPERION BOOKS

NEW YORK

For the home team—Jonathan, Emily, and Pet

First Edition

1 3 5 7 9 10 8 6 4 2

Printed in the United States of America

This book is set in 11-point Palatino.

Library of Congress Cataloging-in-Publication Data on file.

ISBN 978-1-4231-1109-2
Reinforced binding

Visit www.hyperionbooksforchildren.com

He who fights with monsters might take care lest he thereby become a monster. And if you gaze for long into an abyss, the abyss gazes also into you.

—Friedrich Nietzsche,
Beyond Good and Evil

Zombie power for the win!

—MrsKeller

DISCORDIA

Game Manual

FOR THOSE WHO DARE . . .

The eleventh dimension. Beyond your wildest imaginings, yet close as your skin. Nexus of a trillion galaxies and countless forms of life. Birthplace of WorldsWithoutEnd, Ltd.'s latest discovery: Discordia.

For untold centuries, Discordia was a wild and majestic land, sparsely inhabited by clans of herders and farmers. Its monstrous creatures rarely strayed from their murky bogs and dark forests. The people did little harm to one another or to the land. Discordia had no central religion or government; it scarcely had a history. The clans looked after themselves, the druids looked after nature, and every day resembled the one before.

But one young druid—Alchemia Vole—chafed against her ancient order. She was sick of the status quo, tired of tradition, weary of humility and living to serve. She knew in her heart she was destined for greatness; destined for glory—destined to rule.

Alchemia pursued her quest for power in secret, and learned how to use her magic in dark new ways. Her power grew, as did her yearning to rule—yet her druid nature prevented her from taking control. She joined forces with a non-druid chieftain, Lair the Builder, and together they established a new world order. Now Discordia is in turmoil, tainted by gold, greed, and slavery, and controlled by an army of enforcers called the Warriors of Perdition.

Some have grown rich and prosperous under the regime; most have not. Rapid change has tipped nature out of balance, and the druids have been unable to restore it. Fertile fields have turned into wasteland, livestock have grown ill, rivers have been tainted. Monsters have overrun the country, some spreading epidemics with their poisonous breath. Desperate farmers have turned to banditry to feed their hungry families.

But now the oppressed people are striking back. Ordinary folk and druids alike have vowed to restore the old ways of life and to make Alchemia and Lair atone for their crimes. They've organized a fighting force called the Exacters of Penance, and every day they challenge the Warriors of Perdition, soaking the land with blood.

The battles are fierce, and the ranks of both armies are thinning. Disease and death have claimed many. New recruits are in high demand—especially recruits like you: fresh, bright-eyed, and eager to join the fray.

Which side are you on?

WORD OF WARNING

Only fools rush into the eleventh dimension without a manual, and that goes double in the world of Discordia. Why do we say so? Simple. No matter how many Massively Multiplayer Online games you've played, you've never played one like this. Yeah, some things will be familiar: for fifteen bucks a month you'll get to live a virtual life in a computer-generated world. You'll quest, fight, level up, learn a profession, and hang out with other players. But that's just the beginning. Thanks to a huge leap forward in game design, your virtual life in Discordia may seem more real and more exciting than (how can we put this?) . . . real life.

WHAT'S NEW

Discordia is the first MMO to be developed with Realtime Interface Technology™, an innovation that *Gamer Magazine* called, ". . . the greatest boon to gamers since the cable modem." Realtime Interface Technology™ makes it possible for us to customize individual adventures and outcomes just for you, based on your character build and playing style. And if you happen to be questing with friends or fighting in a forty-person raid, RIT will accommodate the entire group.

Just think: a quest you've done three times before is interrupted by a terrible new foe . . . or a temporary combat pet arrives at a critical moment to assist you during a boss fight . . . or you receive an unexpected gift of gold, health potions, or even a Primo—a rare magical weapon or piece of gear. You won't know how, when, or where Realtime Interface Technology™ will strike, but it definitely will, sooner or later.

It's impossible to predict the surprises ahead, yet there *are* ways for you and your group to make the most of whatever happens. (We'll let you in on a few secrets in these very pages.) So do yourself a favor: read before you jump in. The life you save may be your own.

For the extended manual and glossary, please turn to page 224.

chapter one

The problem with killing Wulvers was that, aside from their lupine heads, they were completely human. Their battle cries could only be made by human throats, and they gasped the same way anyone would when MrsKeller's daggers pierced their torsos. The death blow itself sounded with a juicy thump, like a dowel going through a watermelon. Lance had an uncomfortable feeling that the sound effect was based on actual research.

Altogether they had bagged fifteen. The last one was female, and she collapsed at their feet, blood pulsing from her wounds. Lance hated killing the females. Even while dying, the wolf-headed girls looked really good in their buckskin leggings and vests, and he felt like the lowest of the low as he looted their glittering corpses.

He said as much to MrsKeller before the ambush, but she just laughed at him. A Wulver was a *MOB*: a Mobile Non-playable Character. What's more, it was a *hostile* mob: born to be killed.

According to the quest's narrative, Wulvers were infesting

the hill towns of the Borders and terrorizing the farmers and shepherds. The Border Patrol had put a bounty on their heads. Anyone who turned in twelve collars would get a reward from Sergeant Broughampton: five silvers and a chain-mail cloak that gave +5 to strength. With a reward like that, how could killing them be wrong?

MrsKeller had been harping about that cloak for the past hour, and when she realized they had finally killed (and even exceeded) their quota, she cheered once in her shrill, thin voice, then took off. Lance tried to follow her, but the hills were steep, and after three weeks of playing, he still wasn't great at maneuvering. MrsKeller had no problem zigzagging up the slopes, but Lance always managed to choose routes that were impossible to scale, and all he did was run in place like an idiot.

Within thirty seconds MrsKeller was completely out of sight. Lance typed a message, fingers flying over the keyboard. It appeared as blue-letter party chat in the lower left corner of his screen.

LANCE SAYS: LOST! WHERE ARE YOU?
MRSKELLER SAYS: STAY PUT. BE THERE IN A SEC.

A lone zombie sorcerer wouldn't survive long in such a heavily patrolled area. He was sure to be attacked, and his cloth armor couldn't deflect many direct strikes. MrsKeller, a hobgoblin brigand, wore chain mail that could take a lot of pounding. Ideally, she'd make herself the monster's primary target, and Lance would cast his spells from a distance, out of harm's way. If MrsKeller couldn't hold the aggro, they'd die pretty quickly; but that was happening less often now. Their skills were improving and their teamwork was good. This evening was a record: they had completed three quests and hadn't died once—yet.

Lance panned over the alpine landscape. The winter light was dazzling, magnified by snowbanks and a frost-covered path. Somber fir trees cast crisp, dark shadows on the white world, and a single flute played in the distance. The melody ascended to a sustained high note, descended, and ascended again. The pattern repeated many times, yet the flute player was nowhere to be seen. Nothing stirred but three silver birds that circled high overhead.

The birds didn't look threatening, but Lance moved his mouse over one of them to check its stats. The mob was a level 19 Flesh-Stripping Gyrfalcon. He could handle one of them, but not three. He took cover beneath a large evergreen. Could they see him beneath the branches? It seemed likely. Their flight path was widening and lowering, and soon he'd be within their striking range again. He began to type.

LANCE SAYS: COME ON, MRSK. SOME BIRDIES ARE GOING TO HAVE ME FOR DINNER.
MRSKELLER SAYS: FIGHTING.

Lance glanced up at the green line that indicated MrsKeller's vitality. She was losing health rapidly. He knew it was wrong to sit there while she was being attacked, but he was hemmed in on all sides. How could he find her without getting killed himself?

The green line was falling rapidly now.

LANCE SAYS: OH, NOOO. HANG IN THERE, MRSKELLER.
I'M ON MY WAY.

Cautiously he stepped away from the tree. The Gyrfalcons were flying off. He was no longer a target. Perhaps he had never been one.

He ran to the top of a hill and surveyed the countryside. To the west he could see smoke curling from the longhouse chimneys, where the Snow Orcs lived. Beyond the village, newbie orc players were killing their first beasts, level 1 Bears and Ice Leopards. MrsKeller couldn't be there: beginner-area monsters were too weak to challenge her.

Perhaps he should retrace his steps, but where had they even come from? It had started to snow, and their footprints were disappearing fast. He fixed his eyes on the faint depressions, too absorbed in finding his way to be properly vigilant.

A level 22 Plague Beast leaped out from behind a boulder and planted itself in his path. The creature resembled a centaur that had been skinned. Blood pulsed through its body, and a cloud of green vapor surrounded its head. Lance knew that the vapor was a potent weapon: poisonous breath. When the beast was within striking range, it exhaled a lethal green plume that weakened a player's defenses over time.

Lance didn't think he could take it alone. He started to run, and the beast galloped after him. The world around him blurred. The beast's poisonous breath was diminishing his health, but if he could just get to the border of its territory, he might survive.

He ran across a frozen lake, its surface crosshatched by a

group of orc children who were having a skating party. They didn't appear to notice him pass by, though he was close enough to distinguish the light gray spots on their fur hats.

In the distance he glimpsed a road curving around the shoreline. He'd probably be safe if he could reach it. Beasts rarely attacked on major thoroughfares. Those that did were often shot by hobgoblin patrols.

Lance reached the lakeshore and jumped onto the road. The beast wheeled around and ran off as soon as his level 15 Thick Wool Boots touched the frost-dusted cobblestones.

Lance pounded his fist on the desk. *Yes!* He was safe. What about MrsKeller?

He checked her icon. When players formed a group, each group mate was identified by an icon, in the form of a tiny portrait. Beneath the portrait was the character's name and level, as well as a vitality bar that showed their degree of health. When the group disbanded, the portraits disappeared.

MrsKeller's vitality was plunging, and her icon had started to fade. Death was inevitable. Lance watched the vitality anxiously, but to his surprise, it stabilized and began to creep back to normal. He heard the clink of coins going into his bag and heaved a sigh of relief. Not only was she alive, she was looting her attacker—and she had to be nearby or she wouldn't be able to share the spoils.

LANCE SAYS: WHAT HAPPENED?

MRSKELLER SAYS: I SOLOED LITTLE WASHER OF SORROWS!

LANCE SAYS: YOU KILLED A LAUNDRESS?? WHAT NEXT? DRY CLEANERS?

MRSKELLER SAYS: LOLOL. IT WAS A BANSHEE: LEVEL 25 ELITE. YAH!!! HOBGOBLIN POWER FTW.

LANCE SAYS: FTW?

MRSKELLER SAYS: YOU=TRAGIC NOOB. FTW=FOR THE WIN, AS IN THE AWESOMENESS OF MRSK THAT MADE IT POSSIBLE TO KILL WASHER BY HER LITTLE OL' SELF.

LANCE SAYS: WOW. CONGRATS.

MRSKELLER SAYS: ACTUALLY, I TELL A LIE. A LEVEL 58 PENANCE ROGUE DID IT. SHE WAS RIDING THROUGH AND STOPPED TO HELP ME.

LANCE SAYS: PENANCE ROGUE? COULD IT BE AN RIT ASSIST?

MRSKELLER: NAH. SOMETIMES HIGHER-LEVEL PENANCE PLAYERS HELP OUT A BIT, JUST TO BE NICE.

LANCE SAYS: THEY DON'T STEAL YOUR LOOT?

MRSKELLER SAYS: CAN'T, BECAUSE OF DIFFERENT FACTIONS. CAN'T SPEAK TO US OR HEAL, BUT BATTLE ASSIST IS OKAY.

LANCE SAYS: THAT'S GREAT.

MRSKELLER SAYS: YUP. AND THE BANSHEE DROPPED A PAIR OF LEVEL 24 HOBNAIL BOOTS AND A SALT SACK.

LANCE SAYS: A POTION?

MRSKELLER SAYS: NEGATIVE. FIRST STEP OF THE STRANGLEWORM QUEST CHAIN. WE CAN DO IT WHEN YOU'RE LEVEL 20.

LANCE SAYS: NICE OF YOU TO WAIT FOR ME.

MRSKELLER SAYS: YOU ARE NOT WRONG. LOL.

LANCE SAYS: I OUTRAN A PLAGUE BEAST.
MRSKELLER SAYS: SPEEDY ZOMBIE—STAY THERE. OMW.

In another minute Lance saw MrsKeller's tiny figure speeding down the road. She greeted him by bouncing up and down like a tennis ball.

MRSKELLER SAYS: SEE? NO WORRIES. NOW, CLICK ON ME
AND SELECT "FOLLOW" FROM THE PULL-DOWN MENU.
LANCE SAYS: CLICKING, NOTHING'S HAPPENING.
MRSKELLER SAYS: NOT ON ME, YA NOOB. CLICK ON MY
ICON.

He clicked on her icon and got a short menu of commands: "Whisper," "Follow," "Inspect," "Trade," and "Share Quest." He clicked on the "Follow" option, and this time when MrsKeller took off, he stayed behind her like a faithful dog.

LANCE SAYS: THIS IS GREAT. YOU STEER, I RELAX.

MrsKeller stopped running. Automatically, Lance did too.

LANCE SAYS: WHAT HAPPENED?
MRSKELLER SAYS: MURRISKS. DAMN!
LANCE SAYS: WHAT ARE THEY? DON'T SEE ANYTHING.
MRSKELLER SAYS: BAD BOYS. BY RIVERBANK. PLAGUE-
BREATHERS, LVL 20+, PROLLY. WE GONNA BE DEADED.
LANCE SAYS: DEADED? HEH . . .
MRSKELLER SAYS: RUN.

It was too late. Dog-size creatures swarmed up the riverbank. They were veiled in green fog, but when they got closer, Lance could see they resembled rats that were covered with dull gray scales.

MRSKELLER SAYS: EEEEWWW!!!! EEEEK!!!! MRSKELLER HATES THEM! SHE HATES THEM!

The Murrisks charged at the little hobgoblin and tried to sink their mossy teeth into her face. She counterattacked with her two-handed cleaver while Lance cast fireballs, but the odds were against them. Within seconds they were dead, and their spirits were transported to the nearest cemetery. In the game, The Big Sleep was more like a nap, and resurrection was just a few clicks away. Players could buy life at the cemetery, or rez for free by sprinting back to their corpses. Lance assumed they would make the run, though at the moment MrsKeller seemed more interested in jumping on tombstones.

MRSKELLER SAYS: WE'RE SHADOWS OF OUR FORMER SELVES.
LANCE SAYS: ALL MY FAULT. I SHOULD HAVE STARTED WITH A DAMAGE-OVER-TIME SPELL.
MRSKELLER SAYS: NP. WE WOULD HAVE WIPED ANYHOW. TOO MANY OF THEM.
LANCE SAYS: NP?
MRSKELLER SAYS: NP = NO PROBLEM. YOU REALLY ARE A NOOB.
LANCE SAYS: SORRY. TRYING TO LEARN FAST.
MRSKELLER SAYS: YOU'RE DOING FINE.
LANCE SAYS: WANT TO REZ AND TRY SOMETHING ELSE?

MRSKELLER SAYS: SORRY. NO TIME.
LANCE SAYS: C'MON, MRSK, FIVE MINUTES! A FEW MORE
KILLS AND I'LL HIT LEVEL 20.
MRSKELLER SAYS: CAN'T. REALLY SORRY. BIG DAY
TOMORROW.

To demonstrate the depth of her sorrow, MrsKeller used a pre-programmed emote macro to make her shoulders shake. Her sobs were high-pitched and raspy, like a mosquito having an asthma attack. Tears dripped from the yellow tusks that curled out of her nose.

Lance responded with a custom-made emote of his own invention: "The handsome zombie comforts the small green hobgoblin and strokes her luxuriant ear hair."

This made MrsKeller shriek with laughter, and for good measure she hopped up and down.

MRSKELLER SAYS: I'M GONNA REZ AND KEY. NICE GROUPING
WITH YA AGAIN!

She disbanded their group and bought an Instant Resurrection Spell from one of the Cemetery Shades. It only cost thirty coppers, but there was a penalty: fifteen minutes of rez sickness, which diminished fighting power by fifty percent.

MrsKeller was logging out, though, so the penalty didn't matter. She paid the coppers, and as her life force returned, she changed from white to full color. A golden key appeared in her hands and then she vanished.

Lance was alone again. Should he follow MrsKeller's example and key out? He stretched, brushed his hair off his forehead, and looked at the clock—almost four in the morning. His mother would go mental if she caught him playing so late on a school night.

He clicked EXIT and waited the twenty seconds for the game to shut down. Just before it did, he received a dark pink message at the bottom of his screen.

THEGREATONE WHISPERS TO LANCE: GREETINGS, YOUNG SORCERER. AS YOU ARE YET WITHOUT A GUILD, BE AWARE THAT AWOKEN MYTHS IS NOW ACCEPTING NEW RECRUITS. WE ARE AN ACTIVE, HEAVY ROLE-PLAYING GUILD—MATURE PLAYERS ONLY. OUR FOCUS IS ON RAIDS, MUTUAL SUPPORT, AND END-GAME QUESTS. ALL LEVELS WELCOME, BUT SERIOUS, LIKE-MINDED ADVENTURERS ONLY. IF INTERESTED, PSW.

He reread the message, suddenly aware that his eyes were dry and scratchy, as if he hadn't blinked for hours. He didn't know this GreatOne, and no one had been standing near his toon. Wasn't that the only way to whisper to a stranger? He'd ask Finn about it later, at school.

Chapter two

he alarm clock buzzed in his ear like a bee on steroids. It needed to be blasted to smithereens with an Annihilation curse, but that was a level 40 skill. It would probably take months to hit 40—was it 40? It might be 30. That sorcerer in Liander who had told him about the various curses—wasn't *he* level 30? Lance was pretty sure that he was, and he had Annihilate already.

In the midst of these cogitations, it occurred to him that the alarm was still going. He was just about to reach for the snooze button when a purple-robed figure burst into his room and slapped the clock with an open hand. The buzzing ceased, replaced by the sound of someone breathing rapidly through her nose.

Lance looked up at his mother's baleful expression and tried to forestall the harangue.

"Hi," he said. "I'm awake."

"Really?" Her short black hair stood up in spikes, as if she were literally bristling with outrage. "Your alarm's gone off four times already. Of course it's woken me and your father, but you too? I am *amazed*."

He muttered an apology and tried to take refuge under his blanket. She pulled it away from his face.

"Up, up, up. It's a school day."

Lance groaned. "Who cares? I hate this school."

She snapped back. "And whose fault is that? *You've* been determined to hate it from Day One." Lance said nothing. In a softer tone she added, "A midyear move is tough: changing schools, leaving town . . ."

"I know, but—"

"Lance, you'd better hurry." She paused in his doorway. "Just give it a try, okay? Keep an open mind." She sounded so anxious that Lance promised he would, and she turned away with a smile.

As soon as she was gone, he pulled on a pair of jeans and his favorite shirt, a dark blue uniform top with the words "Bill's Garage" written on the back in red letters. He glanced at the clock—should have left five minutes ago.

He raced in and out of the bathroom, shrugged on his ski jacket, and grabbed his backpack. His mother called, "Take some breakfast!" but he was already halfway out the door. His loud "Good-bye" echoed in the hallway.

He raced through the lobby and merged into the crowd outside. At seven thirty in the morning, Lexington Avenue was densely packed with puffy-faced pedestrians who raced along the sidewalks. They only slowed to negotiate the murky slush that pooled at every curb, unwilling to hazard the leap from sidewalk to icy street. Lance usually took the chance and jumped, confident in his long-legged stride and unconcerned about wet feet.

He turned east on 64th Street. He was still half asleep, but he had made good time anyway. There was a chance he'd get to first period before the bell.

A handful of students, motivated by the same goal, were heading toward a shabby brownstone. A small brass plaque identified the building as THE GANSEVOORT; the battered, fingerprint-smudged door identified it as a school.

One of the stragglers was Lance's Discordia adviser, Finnian Ross. Fellow classmate Morgan Frazier trotted at his side, making occasional grabs at Finn's cigarette. He evaded her easily, and took a deep drag.

They all reached the front steps at the same time. Finn gave Lance a quick nod of recognition and exhaled a mouthful of smoke. "How's it going, dude?"

Before Lance could answer, Morgan said, "Put that *out*, Finn. We'll be late."

"Don't sweat it, M.," he told her. "*I* don't."

"Fine." Morgan narrowed her kohl-rimmed eyes. "Stand in the cold if you want. Grow a tumor. Get expelled." She tilted her chin at Lance. "I'll go to chem with *him*."

She grabbed Lance's arm. Finn flicked the cigarette into the street, then jerked his head toward the entrance and raised one eyebrow. Instantly, Morgan dropped Lance's arm and grabbed Finn's instead. They bounded up the steps with him, two at a time. Outside the chemistry lab, they jostled each other, trying to be the first one through. Lance slipped in after them, unnoticed by anyone but the teacher, Lin Ping, who shot him a dirty look.

Mr. Lin darkened the lights for a PowerPoint presentation.

"I'm getting tired of the lateness, people. If anyone's late for tomorrow's test, he"—the teacher glared at Lance and Finn—"or she"—he shifted his gaze to Morgan—"will receive a zero."

Lance sagged in his chair. It was warm in the classroom—too warm. Finn peeled off his jacket and hung it on the back of his chair. He was wearing a T-shirt with the sleeves rolled up to show off his tattoo: a black chain that circled his bicep with the word MACHINE over it in thick letters. He told Lance that he was planning to get a second one of his orc warrior, Mezzukron. His mother swore that she'd cut it from his living flesh if he did, but that was just talk.

Lance fought back a yawn and tried to focus on the review questions, but soon his head began to nod in time with the singsong cadence of Mr. Lin's voice. In another minute he was fast asleep.

Lance walked home with a backpack full of textbooks. He was disgusted. Hours of homework to do, two quizzes, and the chemistry unit test. He barely noticed the gathering clouds until sleet began to sting his face. By the time he reached home, the sleet was giving way to snow.

He went upstairs to the empty apartment, threw his coat on the couch in the foyer, and walked through to the "maid's room," which was now his.

Back in Stirling, he'd had the entire attic to himself. The windows beneath the eaves looked out on a nature preserve, and there was more than enough space for a queen-size bed, two bookcases, and a long utility table where he did his homework.

Now he had been downgraded to his father's childhood bedroom set—a boxy red-maple desk, chair, dresser, and a narrow twin bed—but even kid furniture was too much for this room. If he stretched out his arms he could almost touch both walls.

He cracked open the small window. It faced an air shaft—not much of a view, but the fresh air might help him get through his homework. He turned on his computer. Studying for the chem test would take a while. He'd do the other stuff first—maybe get the essay out of the way.

He looked at the torn gray cover of *Paradise Lost* and then at the glowing Discordia icon. What was wrong with relaxing for a few minutes? He'd be able to concentrate better if he took a little break first.

With one click, the thumbnail-size image of a castle filled the screen. Tattered pennants waved from its crumbling battlements, and the stone walls were tinted with the same bloody hue that darkened the sky.

A tuba section blatted out an ominous fanfare as Lance typed his name and password. With a crash of cymbals, the screen went black except for one trembling mote of green light, exactly in the center of the screen. The tubas started in again, and the mote widened and became an undulating line. The line thickened and morphed into a serpent. The serpent circled around the edge of his screen and stretched out across the center, dissolving into poison-green letters:

Welcome to
DISCORDIA

The message evaporated, and Lance was in. He was standing in the Border's cemetery, exactly where he had been last. He requested resurrection from the Cemetery Shade and accepted the fifteen minutes of rez sickness. He'd be on for half that time—just long enough to visit Liander and check his mail.

He was registered at an inn called the Fangor Arms. As long as he wasn't in battle, a click on his house key would transport him there for free, from any corner of the world. The key required a minimum of two hours' rest after each use, but that wasn't an issue at the moment, since he'd be logging out soon.

He located the key icon on his toolbar and clicked. Instantly he was in Fangor's common room. The air was hazy from a fire that smoldered in the central pit. Perdition characters were sitting on benches near the fire, deep in private conversation. Others stood at the bar, buying gorse-berry wine for thirty coppers a bottle. A few had drunk too much and were dancing on the tables.

A number of characters were standing near the innkeeper, buying or selling trade goods. Innkeepers were Nonplayable Characters (NPCs for short), and functioned as vendors who'd give players their only opportunity to get money for broken teeth, lizard scales, and other trash looted from monsters. Novices assumed that vendors would give them a good deal on everything—a typical noob mistake that betrayed a complete ignorance of Discordian economics. To make serious gold, you had to deal in the open market: the trade channel or the auction house.

Lance had finally figured out how the auction house worked and had put a few things on the block. A number of other players were trying to sell identical items, so he set starting bids slightly lower than his competitors, to encourage bidding. If his auctions were successful, he'd get a note informing him of the final price, and a bag of money from the highest bidder.

He joined the characters who clustered around the innkeeper: a hobgoblin dressed in a long white apron. Lance clicked on him. The innkeeper's welcome appeared in a speech bubble above his head.

"Greetings, Lance, and welcome back to the Fangor Arms. Would you like to buy or sell today?"

Lance clicked "Sell," opened his pack, and unloaded some trash: vulture feathers, broken teeth, boar ribs, and a dented shield. The innkeeper offered him ninety-six coppers—less than one silver. Lance accepted the money and made his way to the front door.

A pink whisper appeared at the bottom of his screen.

MRSKELLER WHISPERS TO LANCE: YOU'RE ON! I KNEW I SMELT SOMETHING ROTTEN.
LANCE WHISPERS TO MRSKELLER: THAT'S DECAY, MY NEW AFTERSHAVE.
MRSKELLER WHISPERS TO LANCE: OOOO. I'M IMPRESSED. ;) WHAT WERE YOU SHAVING?

Her wink made him smile. There was plenty of flirting in the game, but most of it was directed at the hot-looking human characters. Zombies received very little attention.

MRSKELLER WHISPERS TO LANCE: ICK. YOU'RE THINKING WAY TOO LONG.

LANCE WHISPERS TO MRSKELLER: ROFL

MRSKELLER WHISPERS TO LANCE: LET'S TURN IN OUR WULVER QUEST AND FINISH UP THE BORDERS AREA.

LANCE WHISPERS TO MRSKELLER: I'M ONLY ON FOR A MINUTE TO CHECK THE MAIL. :(GOT A %$@LS: @ LOAD OF SCHOOLWORK.

MRSKELLER WHISPERS TO LANCE: THAT'S WEAK, DUDE. THE AFTERNOON IS YOUNG.

LANCE WHISPERS TO MRSKELLER: WISH I COULD. SORRY.

MRSKELLER WHISPERS TO LANCE: KK. BUT TURN IN WULVER QUEST WITH ME. BORDER PATROL HEADQUARTERS IS RIGHT NEAR THE INN. YOU'RE PRACTICALLY THERE.

LANCE WHISPERS TO MRSKELLER: ON MY WAY.

Lance had chosen the Fangor Arms because of its central location in the trade district. Outside, the street was bustling with toons who had business to conduct at the bank, the auction house, specialty shops, or who wanted training in their profession or class. It was difficult to spot the hobgoblin in such a crowd.

MrsKeller saw him first and uttered a high-pitched, nasal cheer. "Perdition forever!"

He responded with a zombie cheer: "Greetings." It sounded

hollow and depressed, but MrsKeller liked it. She blew him a kiss.

MrsKeller whispers: Dude, a random level 60 just offered to run up to four lowbies through Reaper's Horde, in Wealock Prison.
Lance whispers to MrsKeller: Wealock, on Dark Weald Peninsula? Aren't those quests for 40+?
MrsKeller whispers to Lance: Yeah, except for Reaper's Horde. It's an 18+ dungeon. I'm going to ask for an invite.
Lance whispers: Wow. Too bad I can't stay.
MrsKeller whispers: Too late!!! I asked for both already. A 60 can do it in 10 minutes. He'll do the work and we'll get the loot.

A drumroll sounded and a red banner stretched across Lance's screen: "TheGreatOne invites you to a group."

Weird. He was almost positive that this was the guy who'd given him a guild invite yesterday. He clicked "Accept."

Four icons popped up in the upper left corner of his screen: TheGreatOne, level 60 zombie sorcerer; MrsKeller, level 23 hobgoblin brigand; Tikkibar, level 15 hobgoblin rogue; and Excommunitoe, level 16 orc healer.

TheGreatOne says: Welcome, gentlemen and lady.
Excommunitoe says: thx for teh group, dood.
MrsKeller says: Hello, everyone. Thanks, GreatOne.
Tikkibar says: Hi.

LANCE SAYS: HI, EVERYBODY. THANKS FOR TAKING US,
GREATONE.
THEGREATONE SAYS: THE STAR OF FORTUNE SHINES ON EACH
ONE OF YOU THIS NIGHT, FOR VAST RICHES AND UNTOLD
EXPERIENCE AWAIT THOSE WHO ARE BRAVE OF HEART THOUGH
WEAK IN BODY. LET US GATHER AT THE MEETING STONE
OUTSIDE WEALOCK PRISON, ON THE DARK WEALD PENINSULA.
MRSKELLER SAYS: GRACIOUS SIR, WE WILL DEPART THIS
PLACE INSTANTLY AND HEAD FOR THE MEETING STONE WITH
ALL POSSIBLE SPEED.

MRSKELLER WHISPERS TO LANCE: WHAT A NERD. ROLE-PLAYER,
HARDCORE. THIS IS GOING TO BE COMEDY GOLD.

Lance whispered back, "Nerd, yar," but still he wasted no
time adding TheGreatOne to his Friends list. A level 60 who
was willing to help out newbies was an amazing find, and having him on his Friends list meant that Lance would be notified
the moment TheGreatOne logged on. If TheGreatOne was
already playing when Lance joined the game, the Friends list
would show his name and current location.

LANCE WHISPERS TO MRSKELLER: YOU KNOW HOW TO GET TO
THE MEETING STONE?
MRSKELLER WHISPERS TO LANCE: THROUGH LIANDER TO THE
DOCK OUTSIDE CASTLE RUINOS. TAKE FERRY TO DARK
WEALD, THEN FOLLOW PATH TO THE PRISON.
LANCE WHISPERS TO MRSKELLER: SOUNDS DIFFICULT.
MRSKELLER WHISPERS TO LANCE: NP. JUST WALK THIS WAY.

MrsKeller careened around in crazy circles, running through other characters and crashing into walls.

LANCE WHISPERS TO MRSKELLER: C'MON, MRSK. THEY'RE WAITING FOR US! MRSKELLER WHISPERS TO LANCE: SORRY. JOKING. NOW FOLLOW.

MrsKeller guided Lance through the crowded streets of the walled city. Characters were running everywhere, pursuing city quests, buying goods in the shops, getting training, or patronizing the auction house. Many were headed toward the castle at the northeast corner of the city, where a large group had assembled at the docks.

Their timing was perfect. The ferry was approaching. Its dark sides gleamed in the sun, and its carved wyvern figurehead was as menacingly savage as the real thing. Lance had ridden the ferry a few times just to sightsee. He was too low level to accept Dark Weald quests, and the one time he tried exploring on his own, he was jumped by a level 28 Mutant Zombie. The monster killed him and ate his brains, which rather spoiled the illusion.

Now he knew better. He'd stay on the main road until he was under the protection of his friendly level 60 group leader.

The ferry ride was almost too brief to appreciate the scenery. To the south was a view of Castle Ruinos rising above the city walls. To the north across a strait was the Dark Weald and the coastline of the Northern Lands. The ferry pulled in, and everyone ran down the landing plank. Lance clicked "Follow" again, and let MrsKeller lead him down the wide, earthen road that ended at Wealock Prison.

The rest of the group had already assembled at the meeting stone behind the building. Tikkibar and Excommunitoe were sitting on the ground.

TheGreatOne stood a little ways off. Lance clicked the "Inspect" icon to get a close-up of his design and gear.

Like all zombies, TheGreatOne regained strength by eating his victims. Most people played up this ability by giving their toon fangs or blood-encrusted nails. TheGreatOne had none of these personal touches. His toon was an off-the-rack Dry Bones skeleton, without a single moldy limb or maggot-filled eyeball to reveal his personality.

Lance had taken the opposite route. He had wanted to create a zombie double, and had spent more time than he'd ever admit poring over the customization options. Finding the right body was easy: the Fairly Fresh build was appropriately tall and gangly, but the features were more of a challenge. After much effort he managed to assemble a decent-looking face, with a wide, partially intact mouth, prominent cheekbones that poked through gray skin, and a full head of shaggy, black hair. The eye options were all too gross, so he settled on the traditional choice: bright red orbs that burned with inner rage.

The final design was disturbingly good: Lance after a zombie makeover. Impulsively he typed his own name in the character's registration slot. He pressed "Enter," fully expecting to see "Name taken. Try again." Instead, the toon was surrounded with light and heralded with sweet harmonies. Over its head a banner proclaimed, Welcome to Discordia, Lance.

That was that. "Lance" was in the game. It was destiny.

He loved playing the zombie Lance: they shared a physical bond. It didn't seem possible for TheGreatOne to care as much about his generic toon, because he had invested no time creating it. And yet TheGreatOne clearly cared about the game. He had reached the highest level, and he had a full armor set, which was quite an achievement. Some players spent weeks or even months collecting all the pieces, but it was worth it in the end for the extra buffs (magical protection) it gave the wearer.

High-level gear always attracted attention: the cloaks, leggings, gauntlets, and boots came in lurid colors. The breastplates were molded like sculpture, and shoulders and helms sprouted castles, wings, or gargoyles. Lance had never seen a set as dull as TheGreatOne's. His armor was the color of an old dishcloth and had no decoration beyond a meager trimming of clear stones.

Lance guessed that it was one of the designers' inside jokes, and it probably had a funny name, like the Ancient Rags of Albion, or Grime of the Universe. He scrolled over the cloak to check the stats. A long list of benefits popped up, but he read no farther than the label: "Mythic: Legendary Diamond and Platinum Armor Forged with Enchantment." *Primo*.

Whoa.

In disbelief he checked out the entire armor set, piece by piece. No mistaking it: the guy was wearing one of the best armor sets in the game. Maybe *the* best.

And the weapons: the Verdant Wand—another Primo. The Fell Onyx Pole Arm—

THEGREATONE WHISPERS TO LANCE: **WELL MET, YOUNG SORCERER.**

Lance started guiltily, as if he had been doing something wrong. Not that he was. Inspecting another character was perfectly fine—and in any case, TheGreatOne couldn't tell he was doing it.

LANCE WHISPERS TO THEGREATONE: **WELL MET TO YOU TOO. YOUR GEAR IS THE AWESOMEST. THE GAME MUST REALLY LIKE YOU.**

THE GREATONE WHISPERS TO LANCE: **INDEED.**

LANCE WHISPERS TO THEGREATONE: **I'M STILL USING A LEVEL 12 WAND. LOL**

THEGREATONE WHISPERS TO LANCE: **THE LAST BOSS IN THIS DUNGEON, THE EXECUTIONER, OFTEN DROPS A FINE WAND FOR YOUR LEVEL. IF IT DROPS TODAY, IT WILL BE YOURS.**

LANCE WHISPERS TO THEGREATONE: **GREAT!! THANKS SO MUCH. AND FOR RUNNING US THROUGH, TOO. FIRST TIME FOR ME.**

THEGREATONE WHISPERS TO LANCE: **MY PLEASURE. IN MY GUILD, AWOKEN MYTHS, WE ARE SWORN TO FIND AND ASSIST NEW PLAYERS OF YOUR CALIBER, AND HELP THEM HONE THEIR SKILLS.**

LANCE WHISPERS TO THEGREATONE: **DID YOU INVITE ME LAST NIGHT??**

THEGREATONE WHISPERS TO LANCE: **YES. AND THE INVITATION STANDS.**

LANCE WHISPERS TO MRSKELLER: **HEY-HEY, HE INVITED ME TO JOIN HIS GUILD.**

MrsKeller whispers to Lance: Me too. Solid Primos. Check it out.
Lance whispers to MrsKeller: Yar. Something weird, though. He whispered me last night. Stalker?
MrsKeller whispers to Lance: You wish.
Lance whispers to MrsKeller: No really.
MrsKeller whispers to Lance: Who cares. I already joined. We can always leave/ignore if he turns perv.
Lance whispers to MrsKeller: k

Lance whispers to TheGreatOne: I'd like to join. Thank you.

A scroll unfurled in the center of the screen.

"TheGreatOne invites you to join Awoken Myths. Would you like to be an initiate?"

Lance felt a surge of adrenaline. His first guild—and he had been selected by the guild master himself! He clicked "Yes." He whispered his thanks again, but TheGreatOne was talking to the group and didn't answer.

TheGreatOne says: Greetings, my young friends. We are about to enter the dungeon together. We shall go through yonder doorway and descend to the dungeon crypt beneath the castle. Be warned: this is a perilous place. Follow my commands and you will be safe. Any deviation will force me to cast you from the group. Understood?

MRSKELLER SAYS: YOUR WORD SHALL BE OUR LAW, O
GREATONE.
THEGREATONE SAYS: WE SHALL MEET MANY ENEMIES ON THE
WAY TO THE EXECUTIONER'S CHAMBER. I WILL KILL THEM,
AND THEN I WILL KILL THE EXECUTIONER. FINALLY, I
WILL KILL THE REAPER HIMSELF, AND WILL TAKE HIS
SECRET HORDE.
EXCOMMUNITOE SAYS: EXCELLENT.
THEGREATONE SAYS: FOLLOW BEHIND ME AND TOUCH NOTHING
WITHOUT MY PERMISSION. DO NOT ENGAGE IN BATTLE WITH
ANY CREATURE, AND DO NOT ATTEMPT TO HEAL. YOUR HELP
AND YOUR HEALING ARE WORSE THAN USELESS TO ME AND
WILL ONLY SLOW US DOWN. ALL KILLS ARE MINE, AND
WHEN THE KILLING IS DONE, I WILL DIVIDE THE
SPOILS.

In answer, MrsKeller curtsied deeply, and the other characters followed suit, bowing from the waist.

MRSKELLER WHISPERS TO LANCE: OMG, THIS GUY IS A
MASSIVE TOOL.
LANCE WHISPERS TO MRSKELLER: YEAH, NUTJOB. BUT IF HE
GIVES ME THAT WAND, I'LL <3 HIM FOREVER. THE ONE
I'M USING IS ONLY LVL 12.
MRSKELLER WHISPERS TO LANCE: PITIFUL. GOOD LUCK.

TheGreatOne led the group to the prison, a solitary stone building surrounded by pine trees. The entryway was wide enough for the group to pass through, walking side by side.

They walked into the main hall, an empty, echoing cavern that was made of stone from floor to ceiling. Six iron cages flanked the entrance, three to a side. The cages on the right were filled with chained NPC Penance fighters; those on the left were empty.

The wall opposite the entrance was distinguished by five narrow doors containing a swirling oval: the Discordian symbol for a portal. Each portal led to its own dungeon, with singular challenges, mobs, and quests. To enter a dungeon space the group would click on the portal, and the program would generate a copy of the dungeon beyond, for their own use.

TheGreatOne told them to click on the second portal from the left. Lance moused over to the swirling oval and clicked. His screen went black. A few seconds later, he and the entire group were reassembled in a gloomy, torch-lit room. The floor was strewn with bones, and partially rotted bodies hung from the ceiling on chains.

EXCOMMUNITOE SAYS: CREEPY, MAN.
THEGREATONE SAYS: THIS IS THE HALL OF DISCIPLINE.
HEREIN ARE THE REMAINS OF THOSE WHO THOUGHT
THEY COULD GO ON BY THEMSELVES. STAY BACK, AND
LISTEN.

They took the hint and went on without talking. They followed the zombie down a steep ramp that led them into a vast hall with a dais in the center. A narrow door on the far side of the room opened on its own accord, and two empty robes emerged, floating above the stone floor on billows of smoke. The robes drifted around aimlessly, bobbing on an unseen current.

THEGREATONE SAYS: KEEP TO THE SIDE. INCOMING PATROLS.

Tikkibar darted to the center of the hall to get a better look. His sudden movement must have triggered a reaction. The robes froze in place and then transformed into screaming spirits with outstretched talons.

TheGreatOne made a mystical pass with his hands and hit the ghouls with a fiery spell. A battle log to the right of Lance's screen narrated the action like an unseen sports announcer.

THEGREATONE'S FIERY WRATH HITS THE RABID WRAITHS FOR 75 HIT POINTS.

THE RABID WRAITHS CRY OUT IN PAIN AND CALL FOR REINFORCEMENTS.

THE RABID WRAITHS HIT THEGREATONE WITH FLESH CREEP FOR 70 HIT POINTS.

THEGREATONE DEFLECTS FLESH CREEP WITH MIRROR SHIELD.

MIRROR SHIELD REFLECTS FLESH CREEP ON RABID WRAITHS AND HITS RABID WRAITHS FOR 50 HIT POINTS.

THEGREATONE KILLS RABID WRAITHS WITH CURSE OF STRANGULATION.

WRAITHFUL ENFORCERS EMERGE TO AVENGE RABID WRAITHS.

TheGreatOne performs Flay Soul, kills Wraithful Enforcers for 125 hit points.

In less than five seconds the battle was over and the floor was littered with glittering corpses. Excommunitoe darted forward and looted a Wraith that lay behind a pillar.

A message appeared in group chat. "Excommunitoe has been removed from your group."

The orc waved and jumped. He may have been trying to speak to them, but the group could no longer read what he had to say. He tried again in general chat mode, which anyone could read.

"Hey—hey. I'm outta the group. Needa invite." The words were arranged in a cartoon speech bubble. "Invite, invite. Pleez? Won't touch anymore. Peez?"

TheGreatOne ignored him. He looted the corpses and divided the money and the spoils. Excommunitoe went down on his knees and begged.

"Sry, sry. Was accident. Be good from now on. Cmon, d00d."

The group moved on, with Excommunitoe trailing after them, crying loudly.

MrsKeller whispers to Lance: That's cold, man.

Lance whispers to MrsKeller: He did say . . .

MrsKeller whispers to Lance: Yah. Touch nothing! What a nutbar.

Lance whispers to MrsKeller: LOLers.

MrsKeller whispers to Lance: Dang--check out them torches.

Lance shrugged. The torches were ordinary wooden clubs affixed to the wall at a forty-five degree angle, burning feebly at one end. Standard dungeon-issue, he would have said; but when he looked more carefully, he could just make out a writhing yellow and orange figure within the flame.

Excommunitoe ran around them in frantic circles. He brushed up against a wall, and the torch above his head roared and arced through him like a bolt of lightning. His body was consumed in an instant: a smoking pile of ashes was the only indicator that he had ever been there. The light in the corridor was suddenly extinguished.

TIKKIBAR SAYS: I'M BLIND!

THEGREATONE SAYS: PEACE, HOBGOBLIN. LIGHT WILL FALL FROM THE HEAVENS.

Through a small window near the ceiling, bright globes rained down on them, followed quickly by giant moths. TheGreatOne turned them all to stone with a Calcify curse, then invited each party member to loot three corpses of their own choosing.

Lance's drops were nothing special: some wool, a few weak health potions, and a stack of hairy moth legs. A vendor would probably give him less than thirty coppers for everything. The last moth was more interesting: a crate labeled "Lop-eared Rabbit. Bind on equip." He sent the link to MrsKeller.

LANCE WHISPERS TO MRSKELLER: LOOKEE HERE. COMBAT PET???

MRSKELLER WHISPERS TO LANCE: ROFLMAO. LEVEL 1 CRITTER.

LANCE WHISPERS TO MRSKELLER: ?
MRSKELLER WHISPERS TO LANCE: DON'T LOOT IT.
LANCE WHISPERS TO MRSKELLER: WHY?

Lance gave the crate a firm click.

MRSKELLER WHISPERS TO LANCE: U R KILLING ME.

A plump, brown-and-white rabbit emerged. It hopped over to Lance and began to scratch its long droopy ears with its hind feet.

LANCE WHISPERS TO MRSKELLER: WHAT'S IT FOR?
MRSKELLER WHISPERS TO LANCE: ALLERGY ATTACKS LOL.
SOUL-BOUND BUNNY FOLLOWS YOU. BOSSES SNEEZE!
LANCE WHISPERS TO MRSKELLER: HUH. THIS FIENDISH RODENT
WILL MAKE REAPER SNEEZE TO DEATH.
MRSKELLER WHISPERS TO LANCE: BUNNY FTW.
LANCE WHISPERS TO MRSKELLER: DON'T LAUGH. SHE'S STILL
FLOSSING AWAY SHREDS OF THE LAST GUY WHO LOL-ED AT HER.

Light flooded the room. Lance turned around swiftly and saw his father standing at the door with his hand on the light switch. He was wearing one of his "color blind" outfits—an overstuffed red bomber jacket, green pants, and a sky-blue ski cap.

"How was your day?" he asked.

Lance had turned back to the monitor. "Uh-huh," he said in a distant tone. "One second. Gotta concentrate."

TheGreatOne was leading them down a stone staircase that spiraled around a column. It wasn't easy to maneuver. Lance didn't want to fall off the edge, so he kept running into the wall by going too far to the left. He must have looked like a complete idiot, especially since the rabbit was following his moves and looking up quizzically whenever he stopped.

"Lance?" his mother called out. "Have you eaten?" Without waiting for an answer, she added, "Done your homework?"

"One second," he said under his breath.

The stairs were getting narrower and darker. Tikkibar took a wrong step and sailed over the edge. The party chat log noted, "Tikkibar has died." Lance groaned.

"What just happened?" His father moved in closer and stooped down to see the action.

Lance made a shushing sound.

"Was he in your group?"

"Uh-huh."

His mother came into the room and stood next to his father. Lance caught a whiff of sharp, clean, winter air.

"Is Andrew in there?" she asked him.

His father whispered, "Lance said that he hasn't been allowed to play for the past two weeks."

"Why?" she asked.

"He's grounded," his father whispered.

"We only agreed to buy this game to help the boys keep in touch. You'd think the Ellisons would find a way to punish Andrew that wouldn't hurt Lance."

Lance hissed at them. "Quiet! I've got to reach the next boss."

His mother gave a contemptuous snort. "I wouldn't try so hard to get to *my* boss."

"Ma—"

Suddenly the lights went out. Lance stared at the blank monitor.

"No," he said. "I don't believe it. "

"Too bad." His father patted his shoulder. "It's probably the storm. I bet lights are out all over the place."

"My wand," Lance said, pursuing his own concerns. "I can't believe it."

"All is not lost," his mother said. "I have a nice big flashlight with fresh batteries, so you'll be able to finish your homework—even without the wand."

chapter three

The ringing started at five thirty in the morning. Lance peeled his face off the textbook—must have fallen asleep at his desk. He groped around until he located the source of the noise: his phone half hidden under a pile of folders. He pushed these to the floor and jammed the receiver against his ear.

"Okay, then," his father was saying. "I'll tell him. Lance, you on? You have a snow day today."

"What?"

"A snow day. The first one your school has had in sixty years."

"Great," he said, but his father had already hung up.

A wave of relief went through him. Chemistry test postponed. The condemned man gets a reprieve from the governor's office.

He went to the living room window to see what had happened during the night. In the predawn lamplight, Central Park was completely obscured by a whirling fog of snowflakes. Only two people were walking outside, both of them hunched over like battering rams against the wind. A city bus empty of passengers inched along, and a taxi fishtailed across two empty lanes. Its bumper hit a parked car and set off the claxon swoops and honks of a burglar alarm.

Lance thought he might try a bit of cross-country skiing in the park later, when the weather had settled down. Study first? He probably *should* do some more studying, but the rest of his homework was finished. It was almost like a vacation day.

He went back to his room and turned on the computer. He clicked the castle icon. While the fanfare sounded, he typed his name and password and watched the pinpoint of light morph into the line, the snake, and finally the banner:

Welcome to DISCORDIA

A second message flashed: "Please download patch 1.4." Of course. The weekly maintenance. Wednesdays, the game shut down between two and five in the morning to give the designers the chance to fix bugs or add new bits of programming.

He started the download and drummed his fingers on the desk. He didn't have to wait long. This week's patch was unusually large, but the download went quickly. Within a few minutes he was standing in the Fangor Arms.

A bright blue envelope popped up next to his world map. Mail, probably from the auction house. Some of his items must have sold. Good timing. At level 20 he'd have to get new training, and it didn't come cheap.

He clicked on the mailbox outside the inn. Two letters—excellent. Half of his items must have sold. In the first envelope

35

was a purse holding one silver and thirty coppers, for the Elixir of Lionheart. Nice. The coins jingled as they went from the letter to his purse. He clicked on the second envelope. It contained only a note.

He scanned it quickly. Disappointment gave way to shock.

YOUNG SORCERER, A PRIMO WEAPON IS YOURS FOR THE TAKING AFTER YOU COMPLETE YOUR FIRST DUNGEON RUN.

A *Primo*—for him—and all he had to do was get through a dungeon. He needed to join a low-level group right this minute. His fingers trembled as he scrolled through the Groups channel. Plenty of people were looking, but they were all high level. "Come on, come on," he muttered. "Reaper's Horde. Reaper's Horde." Finally he spotted it:

LOOKING FOR GROUP: ONE MORE FOR REAPER'S HORDE. HEALER PREFERRED. PSW.

Lance answered immediately.

LANCE WHISPERS TO ILOVECHUCK: WANT AN ALMOST LEVEL 20 SORCERER?
ILOVECHUCK WHISPERS TO LANCE: SURE. BEEN SPAMMING FOR A HEALER, BUT NO ONE WANTS TO JOIN. WE'LL TAKE WHAT WE CAN GET.

Instantly there was a drumroll and a banner: "Ilovechuck invites you to a group."

Lance clicked "Accept."

LANCE SAYS: HI, EVERYBODY. THANKS FOR THE INVITE!
CARNIVORE SAYS: WELCOME.
STEELMASTER SAYS: HEY DUDE
ILOVECHUCK SAYS: WE'RE WAITING AT THE MEETING STONE.
PSYCHOBETTY SAYS: GREETINGS, LANCE.
LANCE SAYS: OKAY, I'LL BE THERE AS QUICK AS I CAN.
STREETS OUTSIDE THE CASTLE ARE CONFUSING.
ILOVECHUCK SAYS: IT'S EASY. JUST EXPAND YOUR CITY MAP.
LANCE SAYS: ?
ILOVECHUCK SAYS: CLICK ON THE + SIGN ABOVE THE MAP TO
GET A ZOOMABLE BLUEPRINT OF THE CITY. OUR LOCATION
WILL BE FLAGGED. GROUP MEMBERS REPRESENTED BY THE
YELLOW DOTS.
LANCE SAYS: AWESOME! THOUGHT THAT EVERYONE ELSE HAD
GREAT SENSE OF DIRECTION, LOL.
CARNIVORE SAYS: HAHAHAHAHA. THAT IS SO GAU.
PSYCHOBETTY SAYS: IF THAT WAS SUPPOSED TO BE "GAY,"
I'M LEAVING THIS GROUP IMMEDIATELY.
CARNIVORE SAYS: JUST KID. MEANT THATS GAS. SORRY
LONCE.
LANCE SAYS: IT'S FINE.
PSYCHOBETTY SAYS: IF LANCE ACCEPTS YOUR APOLOGY, OK.
BUT I'M WARNING YOU CARN. ONE GAY JOKE AND I'M GONE.

Lance guessed that Psychobetty probably had to leave groups all the time, if this was her standard. The game was rife with people who used the word "gay" as a substitute for "lame," or "newb." Lance had seen this so many times he had almost forgotten it was a slur.

Anyway, he didn't care if Carnivore thought he was a newb. At the end of this dungeon he'd have a Primo. What would Carnivore say then?

He smiled as he turned his world map into a bird's-eye view of the streets. What a difference. He zoomed in close enough to find his own toon, indicated by an arrow in Market Square. He followed a direct route to Monarch's Way, and before long he was on the ferry heading for the Dark Weald. This time he disembarked and found the meeting stone without difficulty.

Many people were milling around, but Ilovechuck, Psychobetty, Steelmaster, and Carnivore actually showed up on the map. Lance walked straight toward them and cheered, "Perdition forever!"

The group had the usual assortment of Perdition characters. Steelmaster and Ilovechuck were level 21 orc brigands with green skin, pugnacious under bites, and chain-mail armor sets. Psychobetty was a level 20 human rogue with hot-pink hair and killer abs, shown to perfection in her bikini top/Daisy Mae armor combo. (Female gear looked as if it wouldn't protect the wearer from *sunburn*, but the stats were identical to the male version.) Carnivore, the level 16 ranger, was doing an Elvis Pelvis dance on the back of his crocodile NPC, Gatoraid. Carnivore wore the badge of the truly clueless: a full set of trash armor (level 9 Hussars) that would be practically useless against the Reaper's Horde mobs. Ilovechuck should have kicked him out, but maybe he couldn't get anyone better.

ILOVECHUCK SAYS: Ok we're going in. Carn, try to stay back as much as possible. You're low for this dungeon, and you'll probably aggro everything.

CARNIVORE SAYS: What u mean?

ILOVECHUCK SAYS: Make all the mobs attack us. They sense the weakness.

CARNIVORE SAYS: kk. letsgo

Chapter Four

$\mathcal{T}$ hey ran into the main hall and gathered at the second doorway from the left. With a click on the portal, Lance's screen went blank. When the graphics returned, he and the others were standing in the corridor to Reaper's Horde.

There was a choice of two routes to the dungeon. Ilovechuck wanted to try the Western Arch, which contained new additions from the latest patch. The opening beneath the arch was narrow and forced them to enter in single file. As each one went through, the entrance grew smaller with a rasp of stone against stone. When the last group member was through, the entrance clapped shut. They were in complete darkness.

CARNIVORE SAYS: YIKES. NOW WE R TRAPED!!!!!!
PSYCHOBETTY SAYS: LOOK!

A single, luminescent ameba appeared in front of them. Its shape shifted constantly, but the light it shed was strong enough to make their faces glow.

LANCE SAYS: IS THAT A MOB?

CARNIVORE SAYS: ???? I ONLY SEE 1.

LANCE SAYS: MOB = MOBILE ENEMY.

ILOVECHUCK SAYS: MOUSE OVER IT BUT DON'T ATTACK YET.

Lance dragged his cursor over the creature: Nightmare Mara, level 25. The ameba solidified and became a ghostly baby swaddled in rags. Its eyes were sewn shut with jagged black stitches, and shrieks poured from its open mouth.

PSYCHOBETTY SAYS: OH HORRIBLE, SADISTIC. HOW COULD THEY DO THIS? AWFUL! I'M GOING TO COMPLAIN TO THE GAME MASTER.

The Mara came closer and revealed triple rows of pointed teeth. Its eyelids twitched madly against the straining stitches, and a curl of smoke drifted from its mouth.

CARNIVORE SAYS: BAD BABY. PERDITION RULES.

Carnivore had his crocodile attack. The battle log opened and began to itemize the details. Lance had just enough time to notice that the Mara cursed Carnivore with a Searing Breath of Pain, before the group exploded with chaotic violence. They buffeted the Mara with arrows, throwing darts, spells, and hammers. Lance hit the baby with a curse of Unbearable Agony—a sorcerer specialty that weakened the enemy gradually, making it easier to kill.

The Mara began to sink under their combined assault. Ilovechuck landed a critical hit with his two-handed axe, and the monster collapsed to the ground.

The group cheered and settled around the corpse to restore their health for the next battle.

LANCE SAYS: ANYONE MIND IF I CANNIBALIZE?

CARNIVORE SAYS: U GO.

LANCE SAYS: NOT THAT HUNGRY. I'LL JUST PICK.

PSYCHOBETTY SAYS: BONE APPETITE.

ILOVECHUCK SAYS: HA HA HA.

Lance clicked on the rib-cage-on-a-platter icon, and his character hunkered down and chewed on the baby's head. His health increased rapidly.

A tiny bell rang, indicating that someone from Lance's Friends list had come on.

MRSKELLER WHISPERS TO LANCE: LAAAAAAAAANCE! WHAT HAPPENED LAST NIGHT?

LANCE WHISPERS TO MRSKELLER: GOT AN RIT LETTER SAYING I'LL GET A PRIMO AFTER NEXT DUNGEON QUEST!!!

MRSKELLER WHISPERS TO LANCE: SOOOOOOOWEEEEEET. CONGRATS.

LANCE WHISPERS TO MRSKELLER: THANKS!

MRSKELLER WHISPERS TO LANCE: WHY'D YOU LEAVE?

LANCE WHISPERS TO MRSKELLER: POWER OUTAGE. BIG SNOWSTORM HERE.

MRSKELLER WHISPERS TO LANCE: HERE TOO.

LANCE WHISPERS TO MRSKELLER: HOW WAS THE REST OF
REAPER'S HORDE?
MRSKELLER WHISPERS TO LANCE: CAKE. TOOK LIKE FIVE
MINUTES, THEGREATONE IS AWESOME. TOTALLY WHACKED-OUT
RP NERD, BUT AWESOME. WHAT YOU DOING NOW?
LANCE WHISPERS TO MRSKELLER: RH AGAIN.
MRSKELLER WHISPERS TO LANCE: YOU FULL UP?
LANCE WHISPERS TO MRSKELLER: YEAH. :(
MRSKELLER WHISPERS TO LANCE: OK. LATER.

Lance realized that his group had moved on. He ran ahead
and saw them waiting for him at the entrance of a vast, damp
cavern. Nothing moved except for the trickles of black water
that dripped down the rocky walls.

PSYCHOBETTY SAYS: SORRY GUYS. HAVE TO LEAVE.
ILOVECHUCK SAYS: YOU JOKING US?
PSYCHOBETTY SAYS: NO.
CARNIVORE SAYS: KK. C U.
PSYCHOBETTY SAYS: BABY'S CRYING. SORRY ABOUT THAT.
THANKS FOR THE GROUP, AND GOOD LUCK.
LANCE SAYS: BYE, PSYCHO. NICE WORKING WITH YOU!
PSYCHOBETTY SAYS: SEE YOU, EVERYONE.

PSYCHOBETTY WHISPERS TO LANCE: I'M ADDING YOU TO MY
FRIENDS LIST.
LANCE WHISPERS TO PSYCHOBETTY: SAME HERE.
PSYCHOBETTY WHISPERS TO LANCE: YOU MIGHT AS WELL LEAVE
TOO. THESE JOKERS ARE NEVER GOING TO MAKE IT.

43

WHOOPS. GTG. BABY REALLY IS CRYING.
ILOVECHUCK SAYS: CRAP!!! CAN'T BELIEVE SHE JUST LEFT
LIKE THAT. CHICKENED OUT, PROLLY. WE MIGHT AS WELL
GO TOO NOW. CAN'T DO THIS WITH FOUR.
CARNIVORE SAYS: WE CAN DO IT. LETS GET REAPER.
STEELMASTER SAYS: I COULD GO EITHER WAY.
ILOVECHUCK SAYS: I GUESS I'M UP FOR IT. WHAT YOU WANT
TO DO, LANCE?
LANCE SAYS: I HAVE A LEVEL 23 BRIGAND FRIEND WHO
MIGHT BE INTERESTED. SHOULD I ASK?
ILOVECHUCK SAYS: HEALER WOULD BE BETTER, BUT OK.

LANCE WHISPERS TO MRSKELLER: STILL INTERESTED IN RH?
SPACE OPENED UP.
MRSKELLER WHISPERS TO LANCE: SURE.

LANCE SAYS: OK. INVITE "MRSKELLER."

The group hunkered down to wait. Carnivore went back to his Elvis dance. Steelmaster and Ilovechuck stretched out on the floor and went to sleep. A string of "zzzz"s came out of their mouths.

Lance surveyed the scene. He was the first to notice the luminescent bubbles hanging from the ceiling. One bubble detached itself from the cluster and floated near them. Its rounded shape took on the outline of a Nightmare Mara. It grew rapidly, twice as large as the first. The details of its face were horribly magnified. A jagged stick forced its jaws apart, and Lance could even see the holes where the thread pierced its eyelids.

CARNIVORE SAYS: **BAD BABY.**
ILOVECHUCK SAYS: **DON'T AGGRO!**

The warning was too late. Carnivore fired his gun, but the bullets caused little damage. The Mara retaliated with fire spells that hurt the entire group. More bubbles drifted toward them, growing and transforming. The Maras formed a circle around the group and began to close in.

LANCE WHISPERS TO MRSKELLER: **RUN BACK.**
MRSKELLER WHISPERS TO LANCE: **ALMOST THERE. HOLD ON. I'LL HELP.**
LANCE WHISPERS TO MRSKELLER: **TOO LATE WE'RE GONNA WIPE.**

ILOVECHUCK SAYS: **FLEE.**

The group broke out of the circle and started to run up the path, trying to get out of the cave. The Maras streamed after them, vomiting fireballs. Gatoraid died instantly, and within seconds Carnivore did too.

Lance kept running, keeping one eye on the group icons. Steelmaster was dead. MrsKeller was alive, but she was under attack. Her health was failing. Ilovechuck was almost dead. Lance couldn't see any of them. He could only see the Maras. One was hovering right in front of his face as if taunting him.

His life was dwindling and he didn't have enough health to use his spells. He took a deep breath and grabbed his knife, the only weapon he could wield without magic. Melee fighting was always the last resort for a squishy character, but he'd have to risk it. He darted forward and attacked with a Slash stroke, then backed up quickly to get out of striking range. He wasn't fast enough.

The Mara hit him square in the chest with a curse of Searing Torment. The pain burned, ripped, and tore. He no longer knew who or what he was, and though he screamed and counterattacked, it was pure reflex. Most of his strikes fell wide of the mark, but one stab pierced the Mara's eye.

Lance felt a whoosh of air against his cheek. The pain stopped, and he knew that the monster was dead. Its body had deflated and lay on the floor like a fleshy puddle, no thicker than a hot-water bottle.

Lance collapsed nearby, unable to move. He wanted to shut down—plunge into complete oblivion—but he was uneasy. There was too much space around him, and the air had a strong scent of earth.

He stretched out his hand and touched damp, cold stone. Was this his floor? He scratched at the surface and felt grit curling beneath his nails. What had happened to the varnished oak floorboards of his bedroom? And why was he wearing a backpack? The thick leather straps pulled tight against his shoulders, pinning him down. He tried to wriggle out of them, but it was too difficult. He was weak and getting weaker. Even though he had won the battle, he was about to die.

It was so unfair. He had held his own—had done amazingly well against all odds. Except for the idiot ranger, he was the lowest level of the group, yet he had done better than any of them—the last man standing. Not that it made a difference now.

His skin chafed against the rough, unyielding floor. He turned his head to relieve the pressure against his cheekbone. As he turned, he saw the Mara and realized he had a choice. He could do nothing and die, or he could use the monster's death to save his own life.

For the briefest of moments he felt divided into two Lances. One Lance was frightened and horrified, but the zombie within had no doubts. The Mara was his.

The frightened Lance was pushed aside, and the zombie took over. Inch by inch he dragged himself toward the Mara. When he was an arm's length away he reached for the flabby body and pulled it to his lips.

His teeth tore through the skin, and a sweet nectar ran down his throat. It was like the essence of angels, better than anything he had ever tasted, better than anything he could ever taste. All the food he loved—charred steak, mashed potatoes covered in a river of gravy, ripe peaches warm from the sun and bursting with sweetness—all seemed dead in comparison, bowls of sawdust and ashes.

He ate and ate until his stomach felt ready to burst. He took one last bite and then sprang up. Energy was surging through him. He had to move—to run as fast as his legs could carry him.

He ran and ran, with no awareness of time, distance, or fatigue. There was a light in the distance. He ran toward it. Soon he saw the mouth of a cave. With one mighty leap he jumped away from the darkness. He lifted his arms to the blinding sunlight, and the zombie within disappeared. He looked at his hands and screamed.

Chapter Five

$\mathcal{T}$ here was blood on his hands. It dripped down his arms and rimmed his fingernails. His cheeks were stiff and coated with stickiness, and there was a metallic tang in his mouth. Fresh blood.

In a frenzy he spat on the ground. Mixed with the saliva were dark black clots. He retched, and his gorge rose violently, as if something alive inside of him was fighting to get out. He fell to his knees next to a rough, stunted tree and vomited blood until he was sure that it was his own blood he was losing.

He was dizzy, confused. So many changes and reverses in a short span of time. He remembered playing the game, entering the game, becoming a zombie—but how could that be? He must be delirious. He stared at his hands. Except for the dark line of blood beneath his nails, they looked the same as ever— the middle and index fingers almost the same length, which always annoyed him. Could those fingers seize a corpse and carry it to his lips? Impossible.

He remembered running tirelessly. He had felt invincible— supernaturally strong. Now he could barely turn his head. He heard a sound like the whistle of an oncoming train. It was a girl running toward him at top speed. Her long dreads streamed out behind her like the tail of a kite, and she was practically screaming her head off.

Lance blinked and looked again. It wasn't a girl after all. It was a boy in a tiny yellow robe that scarcely reached the top of his green plaid boxer shorts. The boy ran up to Lance, pulled his right arm back, and punched him in the stomach.

Lance hit the dirt. He was winded and half-strangled by a swath of rough fabric tied around his neck. A cloak? And why was he wearing this weird tunic and these ragged pants? Where the hell were his clothes?

Someone grabbed him by the neck and pulled him to his feet. Not the maniac in the dress, though. The boy had been jerked to his feet at the same time Lance was.

"Let . . . me . . . go." Lance struggled to turn around, to get a glimpse of this second attacker. A skull looked back at him, a dry white bone with a shred of skin stretched over the cheekbones like a latex glove.

Suddenly the grip relaxed. Lance sat down hard and found himself facing a pair of grayish-white felted boots. His eyes followed the sweep and folds of the robe and cloak and elbow-length gauntlets, all woven from the same coarse, dingy cloth. The primitive garments were strangely at odds with the creature's belt: a silvery chain encrusted with rubies and amethysts, tied at a waist that was no thicker than Lance's wrist.

He paused momentarily—distracted by the jewels—then fixed his gaze on the column of vertebrae that supported the skull. The empty eye sockets seemed to look back at him.

"Thanks for dropping in," the skeleton said, and gave Lance and the boy a jaunty little bow. He waited for a response. None came.

"No, wait a minute—do over." The skeleton raised his arms skyward and intoned, "Welcome to Discordia."

A dry wind tugged at the creature's robe and blew grit into Lance's eyes. He hardly dared to blink, afraid of what the creature might do if he turned away, even for a moment. Lance's body was tense, poised to run or fight, yet nothing happened. The only sound was the skittering of tumbleweeds. Finally the creature lowered its arms and broke the silence.

"Well, *I* thought that was impressive, but maybe you'd like to hear a thunderclap in the background." He shrugged. "Some people are *very* hard to please."

Lance was in a cold sweat, though the sun was high overhead and the air was hot. He looked around for something that would help him make sense of the situation, but he saw nothing but flat, barren land and a mountain range in the distance.

"You're overwhelmed," the skeleton said. "I see that." His sigh sounded like the wind. "I always get the social part wrong. Should I have made the introductions first?"

The skeleton paused as if waiting for an answer, but Lance found himself incapable of making a sound.

"Anyway," he continued, "you two know each other, so there's really no need for formalities."

Lance exchanged a swift glance with the other boy. His vivid green eyes were wide with shock, yet Lance could read the expression perfectly. They had never seen each other before.

"Come on, now," the skeleton said. "Lance? MrsKeller? I thought you were the best of friends."

The boy's dark skin went white to the lips, then he swayed and fell straight back. Lance found himself kneeling at his side without remembering how he had gotten there. The skeleton walked over, but didn't intervene.

"MrsKeller?" Lance's voice shook. Could this be his friend from the game? Was it possible?

Lance tried to lift him to a sitting position, but the boy's head lolled back and forth as if he were dead. "MrsKeller—wake up. Wake up!"

MrsKeller looked bad. Really bad. Lance set him down and anxiously regarded the slack gray face. He grabbed the boy's wrist and tried to find a pulse. MrsKeller's skin was cold and clammy, and he was taking shallow breaths. Could it be shock? Sometimes people died of shock if no one intervened.

Lance tried to remember the proper procedure. Loosen any tight clothing? It was a good place to start. MrsKeller's yellow robe was tight as a corset, and girded with a thick leather strap. Lance noticed a weapon hanging from it, and immediately unsheathed a small, steel dagger. He slit the robe straight down from the collarbone; it fell open in two clean pieces.

MrsKeller took a deep, shuddering breath. Lance rolled him onto his side in case he needed to vomit. MrsKeller's eyes fluttered open. His pupils were dilated so wide that his eyes were almost black, with just a ring of green running around the pupil.

Lance waved his hand to make MrsKeller blink, but instead the eyelids closed.

"MrsKeller, it's me—Lance."

A shadow spread along MrsKeller's face. Lance turned and was astonished to see the skeleton kneeling down near MrsKeller's head. In his panic Lance had forgotten all about him.

The creature pried open one of MrsKeller's eyes and made a clucking sound. "Well, this will never do." He opened a brown suede purse that was hanging from his belt and rummaged among the contents. "Let's see . . . Hmm." He took out a flat clear flask, pulled out the cork with his teeth, and tipped the bottle upside down.

"What's that you're giving him?" Lance had a wild urge to smack the bottle away.

"Shhh," the creature said. "Patience." He tapped the glass as if he were trying to get ketchup out of a new bottle. After a moment, a drop of viscous liquid collected on the rim. The skeleton opened the corner of MrsKeller's mouth just in time for the drop to fall into it.

"What is that?" Lance repeated.

"Just a little health potion."

MrsKeller instantly opened his eyes and saw the skull hovering over him. With a shriek, he yanked at the corner of Lance's cloak and pulled it in front of him like a shield.

"Get away from me, monster," he said. "I'll . . . I'll cut you." MrsKeller's right arm reached down for a weapon, but then he stopped and looked confused.

The skeleton stood up and shook his head slowly. "MrsKeller, you don't look at all well. Pull up a bit of Wasteland and get comfortable. You too, Lance."

Lance sat down hard. The skeleton continued.

"Needless to say, I'm TheGreatOne. Level 60 zombie sorcerer."

"Oh my God," said MrsKeller.

TheGreatOne positioned himself in front of them as if he were onstage. "So," he said, "welcome, guildies, to the first meeting of Awoken Myths. Technically, there ought to be at least ten members here, but when only one in a million can qualify, we can't be too particular about the *rules*." He laughed, making a sound like sticks tumbling down a flight of stairs.

"Our first meeting is supposed to be a friendly get-to-know-you session, so let's be informal." With a flourish, he placed his right hand where his heart should have been. "Call me G.O. if you prefer to be casual, or GreatOne, or T.G.O.—it's all good." He paused for a moment "Just don't call me 'Go.' It would sound like you wanted me to leave."

He laughed once more, although neither of the boys joined him. The zombie looked disappointed.

"I must say, you two are not very talkative. I thought you'd be more excited, considering how much you like to play."

Lance rubbed his eyes. "Are we actually in the game?"

"The colors are wrong," MrsKeller said in an undertone. "It's all changed."

"The colors?" Why was MrsKeller worried about colors at a time like this?

"In the game?" The zombie waggled an admonitory finger. "Magicked into a piece of software? Please!"

"If we're not in the game," MrsKeller said, "where are we?"

TheGreatOne began to laugh. "You're in Discordia, of course.

Eleventh dimension, worlds without end, welcome to it, and so on and so forth." He stretched out on the ground, propping himself up on one elbow.

"In Discordia?" MrsKeller's voice trembled with suppressed emotion. "Are you mental?"

"Use your eyes, MrsKeller." The zombie swept the air with his spare hand. "Observe the blasted landscape of the Wasteland. Look behind you and see the cave through which you exited Reaper's Horde."

MrsKeller and Lance turned around hastily but saw nothing but a mound of dark stone.

"It's a trick," MrsKeller said. "That's not a cave."

"True," the zombie conceded. "At least, true for the moment. Things work a bit differently here."

"So it's not the game." MrsKeller said flatly. "It just looks like it."

"Correct. This is the world that inspired the program. It's not an exact copy." The zombie suddenly turned defensive. "I never said it was. Even if I had *wanted* to create a mirror image, I couldn't, because of the team. They wanted to add all kinds of garbage." In a confidential tone he said, "Those orcs and hob-goblins were not my doing, I can tell you. *So* trite. They wanted elves too, if you can believe it—they love designing the girls— but I had to put my foot down. Elves—I ask you . . ." He shook his head. "Anyway, they had their fun designing little outfits for the human girls: the skanky push-up breastplates, chain-mail hot pants, iron bustiers—and if you only knew how many 'jokes' I endured about level 60 boobs . . ." TheGreatOne said this with the air of someone who would roll his eyeballs if he only had the means.

Lance swallowed hard. "What about the other stuff. The monsters . . . and the zombies?"

TheGreatOne's tone became evasive. "There've always been *some* monsters here: traditional creatures that I recognized from Celtic stories—"

"And zombies?" Lance persisted. He didn't want to hear about other creatures now.

"Well . . ." TheGreatOne began to drum his fingers against his jawbone, stalling for time. "How can I put this?" He paused for a moment, and then began, "The thing is, putting zombies in the game was my idea. They had nothing to do with this world, but I've always loved them—in movies, you understand. And all the games have a zombie race, so what was the harm of using them again. I thought it would be fun to see them running around in the program."

Lance knew that TheGreatOne was holding something back. "So what happened to you, then? You sure look like one to me."

"Ah." The zombie's drumming began to speed up. "That's a bit of a puzzler. I *am* a zombie at the moment, but that has nothing to do with the game. Nothing at all. Sheer coincidence." He sounded as if he were trying to convince himself. "You see, I had been visiting for a long time already, and I was completely myself whenever I dropped by for a visit. But once I started the game design, my visits changed. I began to develop new abilities: magical power, like the druids. It was fun at first, but then things changed. Just imagine—" he said, "I'd drop by for a little fishing and suddenly find myself climbing a mountain, or destroying a stone wall, or setting fire to a field. Not because I wanted to do such pointless things: I had no choice.

My actions were controlled by someone else: I was a toon."

MrsKeller seized on this immediately. "So you're a toon now? A minute ago you said everything's real here."

"Must you be so prosaic?" The zombie sighed heavily. "I'm talking about *feelings*, MrsKeller. I was worried. At times I even doubted my sanity."

MrsKeller's only response was a faint snort. The zombie ignored it.

"I seriously considered staying away, but I hated giving in to fear. I decided to learn the cause of this transformation and then destroy it."

"Oh, yeah?" MrsKeller jabbed the air with his index finger. "How'd you plan to do *that* if someone was controlling you?"

The zombie pointedly ignored him now and addressed his comments to Lance. "The change only took over once in a while, and whenever I could I sought the answer to the mystery. After much effort I traced the problem to Alchemia. Once she began to use new magic here everything changed. Sometimes I could control my powers, and sometimes they controlled me. My mind was increasingly compromised, and my body began to wither and lose flesh. Eventually I was nothing more than a walking skeleton"—he paused dramatically— "a *zombie*." In an ordinary tone he added, "I was not pleased."

Lance felt a tiny burst of sympathy, in spite of himself, yet he also had some doubts. TheGreatOne was clearly too willful to be subject to another. Lance eyed the skeleton, trying to picture him as the sorcerer's victim, unwillingly raised from the dead. "You're really a zombie? You've cannibalized things?" To his horror, he felt his mouth water.

The zombie waved this away. "That's a zombie ability in the game. In the real Discordia, zombies don't act that way. I should know: I'm the only one."

To himself Lance added, *Make that two.*

"I see what you're thinking," TheGreatOne said, misinterpreting Lance's expression. "Life may indeed copy art, if Alchemia gets her way."

"So she's creating zombies?" Lance said.

"Certainly. A certain class of person *always* tries to raise a zombie army, though in Alkie's case 'try' is the operative word. But let's be charitable. She's trying. It's all experimental magic—entirely new—and the technology seems to be way over her head. Her first attempts have been a disaster."

Lance breathed a sigh of relief. "I'm surprised she even tried it."

"Ah." The zombie's eye sockets flashed red. "I didn't mean to imply that she failed. Just the opposite. But the problem was, she only used parts."

MrsKeller interrupted. "Parts of what?"

TheGreatOne turned on him. "The woman blunders around unleashing forces she can't control—forces that are wreaking havoc on me, a perfectly innocent bystander, and *then* she decides that it would be a good idea to start small."

MrsKeller waited for the answer. "So?"

"Do I have to draw you a picture? She's created zombie *limbs,* and she doesn't know how to control them. She's a destroyer, and if we don't stop her, she'll ruin everything good in this world. Zombies are just the beginning."

MrsKeller leaned closer to Lance. "Guy is nuts. 'We'?"

"I *heard* that, MrsKeller, and maybe you're right. It does

seem crazy to select anyone as dreary and ordinary as you and
Lance. Naturally you must wonder what you could possibly
have to offer."

"We weren't thinking *that*," MrsKeller said. "Me and Lance
have *plenty* to offer."

MrsKeller looked as if he wanted to kick the skeleton into
the sand, and Lance nodded his head vigorously to show that
he was behind MrsKeller all the way—though in truth he
wasn't too sure about his own qualifications.

"You must be asking yourselves how I managed to find you
in the first place. And the answer? Through the game, of course."

"The game?" MrsKeller looked up sharply. "How?"

The zombie chuckled. "Discordia is a nice little MMO, and my
Realtime Interface Technology is rather elegant in a small way,
but it's nothing compared to its real purpose." The zombie
leaned forward. "Which will be our little secret, of course."

Lance was sure he was dreaming this conversation. It had all
the logic of dreams—when wildly improbable and bizarre
events occur but no one seems surprised. He heard MrsKeller
mutter, "Nutbar."

"MrsKeller," the zombie said coldly, "after all the trouble I've
taken to find you—countless hours of planning, calculating,
experimenting—so much work that had to be done in secret,
and worked into the program design without anyone being
suspicious . . . and do you know why, MrsKeller? Do you?"

"Er," MrsKeller acted as if he were defusing a land mine.
"Not really."

"Pah! Not *really*." TheGreatOne clasped his hands behind his
back and began to pace with short, clipped strides. "Not at all,

you may as well say. You have no idea what I've done—what I've achieved." He stopped pacing and drew himself up. "This little game, this Discordia, is a ruse, a blind, a net. Yes, a beautiful net."

Lance echoed "A net," yet he was mystified. What was TheGreatOne going on about?

The zombie seemed to hear the unasked question. "It's a metaphor, Lance. I'm using the game to help me sort through the players. I've designed a program within a program, to analyze how players solve problems—particularly how they approach my special little roadblocks. It alerts me whenever it finds a promising subject, and then I observe, hoping to find people like *us*." TheGreatOne rapped on his femur for emphasis.

"What do you mean, people like us?" Lance said. "We're not like you at all." He spoke angrily, but inside he felt cold. Did TheGreatOne assume that they were like their characters? That Lance was harboring a secret wish to curse people with painful spells, watch their agonized death throes, then eat them while they were still warm?

TheGreatOne seemed surprised. "But you *are* like me. And I've been watching and waiting for you a long time. People with our abilities don't appear every day."

"What abilities?" MrsKeller gave a contemptuous snort. "We're not even level 25 yet."

A faint red glow pulsed in TheGreatOne's eye sockets. "Obviously not gaming abilities. If I wanted to find that, I'd have millions of better choices." He gave an exasperated sigh. "The ability I'm talking about is so unusual that you've never heard of it." He put his hand up to forestall their questions. "I really can't go into it now. I may not have much time."

"Spit it out already—if that's possible." MrsKeller was practically vibrating with rage and frustration. "What's the plan? Why do you need our so-called *ability*?"

TheGreatOne wagged an index finger in MrsKeller's face. "Temper, temper, MrsK. I was about to explain. I've invited you to group: a real group, in the real Discordia—and the quest . . ." He trailed off. "Real excitement ahead, but I can't do it solo. Now, though, with your abilities—"

Lance swore, "Whatever they are, you can't make us use them."

"Too late." TheGreatOne slapped his bony knees. "You've done it already, just by showing up, and that sets you apart from just about everyone else. Most people would love to help me, but they can't. Their brains no longer have those connections; they lost the ancient pathways. But you, MrsKeller"—he inclined his head respectfully—"and you, Lance"—he bowed again—"are special. You have the *ability*."

MrsKeller shouted, "What—to be summoned here? To be your slave?"

"If that's how you want to see it," said the zombie, "though why be so negative? It's a glorious thing, and we all share it: you, and I, and our associate, Lance. We can slip into the eleventh dimension, where there are worlds without end. And now, with your help—"

"Forget it," Lance said. "We're leaving." TheGreatOne slowly got to his feet. His arms drifted upward, straight in front of him like a sleepwalker's. He glided toward them and murmured, "Accept. . . . You . . . have . . . no . . . choice." His voice was drained of emotion. "You don't know how to get back."

CHAPTER SIX

heGreatOne's eye sockets filled with red light, as if someone had pressed a switch. "Changing. You must help. Stop. I. Need me . . ." He rose to his feet, uttering a stream of disjointed syllables. He turned toward the cave, but the mouth had closed, replaced by solid rock. The skeleton hurtled toward it with outstretched arms.

MrsKeller screamed, "Stop!" but the zombie ran on. Lance braced himself for the crash and an explosion of splintered bone. Instead, the rock face swirled and softened. Still gabbling, the zombie stepped into the rock as if entering a pool of water. Bit by bit its body submerged and disappeared, and the voice cut off midsyllable.

"It's a portal," Lance yelled. "He's gone through!"

They raced to the spot where the zombie had disappeared, but the portal was gone. The cave had sealed over without a single crack or line to mark where the entrance had been.

Lance pushed the surface with both hands, willing it to become permeable again. It didn't budge. With a howl of frustration he hurled himself against it and felt a wave of pain go through his shoulder. He went back to pounding with his hands.

A tremor rumbled beneath him as if the A train were going by. MrsKeller grabbed Lance's arm and pointed to a rapidly moving shape.

"Incoming!"

Lance wheeled around. "Where?"

Another tremor shook the ground violently. The air was filled with a harsh, cawing sound, and there was a stink of roadkill rotting in the sun. They clapped their hands over their noses and mouths, and ran. Beneath their feet, the desiccated earth crackled into a mosaic of dun-colored fragments. Deep lines became cracks and fissures, or opened into chasms—first small ones that they could leap over, then wider ones that they didn't dare attempt.

The fetid smell pursued them, and the roaring grew ever closer. Heat rose at their backs until it was almost unbearable. In a blind panic they ran onward toward an enormous red plateau. It probably stretched out for a mile: there would be no way around it.

MrsKeller pointed to a dark horizontal gash in the plateau's rough surface. It might have just been a shadow, yet he hurled himself at the darkness, and disappeared. Lance followed and found himself wedged into a small cavern that ended about ten feet from the rock face—close enough for them to be sitting ducks for whatever was out there.

They wriggled as close to the cavern entrance as they dared, and looked outward. A dragonish creature as big as a school bus was running back and forth on two thick, stubby legs. Part of its tail had been chewed off, and the ragged stump was rotten with pus. Leathery wings extended from its sides like a hang glider. Every so often a gust of wind buoyed the creature aloft for a short distance.

Suddenly the creature froze: it had caught their scent. With slow deliberation it flattened itself against the ground and crept forward on its belly. As it moved, its head shifted from side to side as if trying to get them in focus, and with every step, the heat and stench of its carrion breath grew stronger.

A scaly leg shot out to pull them from their shelter, but the entrance was only wide enough to admit three curved talons. Lance flung himself backward, squashing MrsKeller against the wall.

The creature tried reaching in with the other leg, and was equally unsuccessful. Frustrated, it pressed its jaws to the rock face and snapped down hard. A chunk of stone gave way, partially blocking the cavern. The creature roared and bit down harder, getting another mouthful of rock. The boulder shattered beneath the force of its jaws. With a piercing shriek, it drew back and slammed itself against the cliff. The impact sounded like a wet towel hitting a wall. The stunned creature sank to the ground.

"You think it's dead?" MrsKeller's whisper made Lance start so violently that he smacked his head on the stone above him.

"Dead?" Pain made Lance's voice sharp. "Just knocked itself out, probably."

MrsKeller winced. "You and the monster, both. Must be something in the water. I'm Adam, by the way."

"Adam?" Lance touched his head gingerly, half expecting to

feel scales or feathers instead of skin. *"Adam?* And you play *Mrs*Keller?"

The boy laughed. "Yeah. Adam Boudreaux." He stuck out his hand.

Lance shook it and muttered, "Lance Taylor." His eyes were fixed on the prone creature. "At least I used to be. Now I'm not sure."

"I know what you mean."

They crawled out of the cavern and took a few steps toward the festering stump. Rivulets of yellow ooze ran down the uneven surfaces and collected in a puddle. "In the game," Lance said, "we'd last about two seconds if we aggroed a Wasteland Wyvern."

"Here, too," said MrsKeller. "If it was healthy."

There was an awful pause while they contemplated the patch of scorched earth beneath the wyvern's mouth.

"I suppose there's more," Lance said in a deliberately neutral tone.

MrsKeller shaded his eyes and scanned the horizon. "Don't see any others out, but then again, I didn't see this one until it was right on top of us. Maybe they have holes in the ground."

"Around Reaper's Horde?" Lance felt the hair on his arms stand on end.

"Could be anywhere, really."

"How will we get back?" Lance asked.

"Don't know if it matters. That crazy zombie ran off on us, and Reaper's Horde seems to be gone."

Lance slumped back against the plateau. The world had been replaced by a dead, empty land, and the only way out had slammed shut. Where could they go now?

He looked at MrsKeller's face, expecting to see a reflection of his own despair. MrsKeller, though, had his back to him, absorbed in his own thoughts.

"We should probably head east," MrsKeller said distantly. "If this place is laid out like the game, east is our best bet." He squatted down and traced a square in the dirt. "Look here. This square is Reaper's Horde, okay?"

Lance bent down to look. "I'd recognize it anywhere."

"On our map, east of R.H. is the Red Plateau." He drew an oval. "Here."

Lance rapped his knuckles against the red stone behind him. "And here?"

MrsKeller nodded. "The eastern side of Red Plateau is a lowbie questing area."

"You're sure? I don't remember doing any Wasteland quests."

"Sure we did," MrsKeller said. "There's a mountain range that divides the Wasteland from the Borders. You cross over this twin-peaked mountain—Saddleback Mountain—and on the western side you're in the Wasteland. Don't you remember the Starved Cougar quest—the big old mama cougar with the three cubs? She must have killed us five times before we figured out that if we killed a cub first, its health was automatically transferred to the mama."

It came back to Lance and he remembered how infuriating it was. "Maybe we'll see some starving cougars here, too."

"No problem," said MrsKeller. He pretended to peer down the sights of a rifle. "We know how to deal with them now: kill the mama first, then head for the hills."

chapter seven

R ayva crouched next to the deer beneath the dripping branches of a white pine tree. Except for the weather, she had been very lucky. The doe had wandered right in front of the blind, no more than fifteen feet away. Rayva's first arrow went through its neck, severing a blood vessel. The animal panicked and bounded off, but the effort just made it hemorrhage faster.

The maddened doe left a trail of blood: on the ground, smeared on trees, splattered on plants. Clumps of crushed vegetation showed that the deer had fallen but had managed to get to its feet. It struggled as long as it could, and when its strength failed, it crashed to the ground.

When it saw Rayva approach, knife in hand, it made one convulsive effort to rise. Its legs stirred feebly and its body trembled until Rayva ended its suffering with a merciful slash across the neck. Rayva waited until its eyes went dull before wrenching the arrow free. Then she grabbed its front legs and pulled it to one of the small streams that ran into Dead River. The water was still good here, and Rayva had frequently drawn drinking water near this very spot.

The storm began just as Rayva was preparing to butcher the deer. The rain on her face felt like tears, and the forest grew dark—too dark to work safely. She'd have to wait it out, miserable, cold, and all too aware of how much more work she'd have to do before she could rest.

She dragged her sleeve against her face. Crying wouldn't help. She idly used her thumb to test the edge of her skinning knife. It was sharp enough to part a few layers of her skin. It would be easy to open the artery that ran from her wrist to shoulder. She'd bleed out within minutes, and it probably wouldn't hurt much—not that she'd ever try such a thing. She always dreamed of escape, but never that way.

She shook off these thoughts. Finally the storm clouds were pushed south by a cold northern wind, and Rayva could finish her work. It was best to do the skinning while the carcass was warm. It still retained the integrity of a living body, with individual parts that could be separated one from the other. A cold carcass was rigid, and fought against the blade.

Rayva rolled the animal onto its back, propped it up with some large stones, and tied one hind leg to a sapling. She gripped the elk-horn handle of the skinning knife and made short cuts up the abdomen, starting from the pelvis. The cuts were shallow, just deep enough to slit the hide and stomach muscle. A plunging stroke would pierce the intestines and ruin the meat.

Next she worked her knife around the rectum using the same short, shallow strokes until the tubelike colon separated from the surrounding tissue that had anchored it in place. She quickly tied off the end to prevent the contents from leaking, untied the leg, and rolled the carcass to its side, allowing the coils of the intestines and other organs to spill out onto the ground. It was neatly done; even the bladder had remained intact and hadn't fouled the meat.

With the lower organs clear, she began working on the upper body. She felt for the diaphragm, which separated the organs of the chest from the abdomen, and cut through it. Then she reached up with her knife as far as possible into the deer's chest. With her free hand she grasped the esophagus and windpipe and sliced through them with her knife. One firm tug and the windpipe and esophagus were free, followed by the heart and lungs.

Most of the outdoor work was done now. She left the loops of intestines for the wolves, but took the organ meats. She gave them a quick rinse, popped them into linen sacks, and placed them back inside the deer.

Rayva plunged her arms and face into the icy water of the stream. She scrubbed her skin with handfuls of moss, rinsed again, and shook herself dry. The chill sank straight into her bones, but as soon as she lifted her kill, she'd be warm—far too warm.

To make it easier to carry the carcass, she punched a hole in the lower jaw and the hind legs, then passed a rope through each hole and pulled tight. When the head and legs touched, she knotted the rope firmly. Now she could wear it like a sling: neat and secure.

Even so, it was a heavy burden. Sweat poured down her face and blurred her vision, and the skin on her neck quickly became raw. Her legs trembled under the weight of the deer, and she wondered for the hundredth time why all the good people ended up slaves, and the bad ones villagers.

Villagers seemed to have all the luck. Her keepers, Sal and Arabis, had two slaves to do the chores, and now they talked of getting an "indoor" slave for their beloved daughter, Aster.

Aster did no work at all, but they thought it would be a fine thing to have a slave to dress her hair, tend to her wardrobe, and do everything possible to keep her plump, blooming, and lovely. Nothing was too good for her.

Aster had just turned fifteen, and Rayva guessed that she herself was probably the same age, though she couldn't be sure. Her past was a blank. Arabis often said that Rayva's people were filthy rogues who robbed and cheated honest folk until the Warriors of Perdition finally rounded them up and forced them into slavery.

Was it true? Could she really have come from a rogue clan? She *did* understand weapons and hunting—but that didn't prove anything. Rangers were equally famous for their woodcraft. Perhaps she had belonged to one of the ranger clans with Penance sympathies, but Arabis didn't want her to know the truth: the knowledge might feed rebellion. Better to say that Rayva was nothing more than a base, despicable criminal.

Rayva's memory began at the Narduk slave fair, two winters ago. Her earliest recollection was of sobbing children calling for mothers and fathers who weren't there, the stunned faces of the older folk, the shrieks of protest when the Warriors closed the prison collars around their necks.

The collars were imbued with a simple boundary enchantment, which allowed the slaveholder to put limits on the slave's movement. Any attempt to set foot outside the stated borders, and the collar tightened in a choke hold, to the very death if necessary.

Rayva was allowed to roam throughout the forest. She knew every inch of it, and could find her way back with her eyes closed, just from the smell. The stench that hung over Seyre was so strong that unwary travelers often reined in their horses as if stunned by a blow across the face.

The main culprit was the tanning yard by the river. Water was essential to the tanning process, and the Seyrens used it to fill the soaking pits and carry away waste. This rendered the water unfit for any other purpose. No fish lived downstream of the tannery, and the villagers had to get their drinking water elsewhere.

The bridge that connected the forest to the village led straight through the tannery, but Rayva tried to avoid it. She hated watching the tanner slaves working the soaking pits and the scraping tables, but most of all she pitied the poor slaves who had to soften the hides with warm dung.

Today she was too tired to take the long way around. She paused at the bridge to unknot the scarf she wore around her neck, and tie it over her nose and mouth. She trudged across the bridge and into the yard, nodding to anyone who looked up, and continued onto the main road through the village.

The old part of town came first: clusters of mud-and-straw hovels that gradually gave way to larger, wood-framed homes. All loyal citizens—and everyone in Seyre considered themselves such—had been promised one of these marvels. Some had as many as four rooms, with a separate little house for the poultry and livestock.

Seyren families often gathered at the site of their new homes, and Aster never missed a day. She claimed to be very interested in the process of building, but Rayva knew that she only went to flirt with the brawny workers.

To Rayva, the new house meant that she'd have to lug the deer for another ten minutes—nothing more. As it was, she was so tired that she considered the skinning shed a welcoming sight.

She ripped off the scarf and dumped the carcass on a long table. The sudden relief almost made her lose her balance. She rested against the table until she felt steadier, then grabbed the bundle of organs and ran outside.

Rayva burst through the door of the cooking shed, startling the elderly woman who stooped over the fire.

"Mercy, child. You'll be my death, coming in like that."

"Sorry, Vered. Just have to give you these." She held out the bundle.

The kitchen slave put the meat in a basin but kept her eyes on the girl. "Hard day?"

Rayva shrugged. "No more than usual." It wasn't true, but she didn't want to encourage Vered's grumblings: the older slave could complain for hours. Rayva tried to change the subject. "Where is everyone? I didn't see a single villager."

"A town meeting, girlie. There've been rumors of strangle-worms in one of the streams."

"Never heard of such a thing," Rayva said.

"That's because they haven't been seen in the river for many years. They're horrid creatures, halfway between an eel and a garden slug, but they can grow as big as you."

"What a frightful combination," Rayva said absently. Her mind was on the skinning. "I'd better get back to the shed."

"You sit for a few minutes and have a cup of tea, and then the work will go faster."

The old woman poured a steaming liquid into a hollow gourd. "Drink that," she said, pushing it into Rayva's hands, "and I will tell you about the worms."

Rayva gave in. "I can only stay a minute." She cupped her hands around the thin sides of the gourd and felt the warmth go through her fingers. She inhaled the steam and closed her eyes, listening to the music of Vered's soft voice. Then she caught the meaning of the words, and all peace fled.

". . . and if they get hold of you, they'll likely drag you underwater and squeeze you to death."

Rayva covered her mouth.

"And it gets worse." The slave was warming up to the grim tale. "They say a plague beast is roaming on the other side of the forest. At first sight it might resemble a man on horseback, yet it's one creature, and it breathes a sickly air that spreads disease from one person to another. And if it breathes right on a person, they'll die within a few minutes."

"Why have they come back after so long?"

"That is the important question, isn't it? The druids used to keep the beasts confined on a little island somewhere. Of course, they did escape from time to time, but mostly not. But now—with all the druids having gone to the

Northern Lands—there's talk of a new infestation."

Rayva turned this over in her mind. "Serves the villagers right then, for driving off the druids."

"Hush, child!" Vered said in alarm. She lowered her voice. "It's true, of course, but it's treason to say so."

Rayva sighed. "Life must be better there, where the druids are."

Vered nodded vigorously. "Best not to speak of it," she said in a low voice. "There's evil all around since the sorcerer came—she may be listening even now."

"Listen *here*?" Rayva jumped up and knocked over her cup. Tea slopped on the table. She grabbed a rag to clean it up, but Vered took it from her hand.

"Run along," she said. "Finish the skinning and come back to visit when you're done."

"I will." Rayva put down the rag hastily. "Thanks for the tea." She ran out of the kitchen.

The door to the skinning shed was ajar, and the deer was just where she'd left it, head lolling off the table. She approached it mechanically, face rigid with exhaustion, and braced herself for the final effort.

She pushed an iron rod through the holes in the hind leg and hooked the rod to a pulley. Hand over hand, she hoisted the deer to the rafters and tied the rope to a winder's hook. She shoved the table against the wall to get it out of the way.

She had to concentrate now: rush the skinning, ruin the pelt. She closed her eyes and pictured the inner architecture of the animal—skin and muscle separated by a protective membrane. If she respected the integrity of this barrier and avoided cutting into the meat, she could peel away the skin in the same way she'd peel a grape.

She made a cut down each leg and placed the knife on the table. Most of the next part was done better without it. With her fingers and thumbs she separated the hide from the meat of one leg and then the other. The muscles stayed clean, encased in translucent membrane. She continued down the spine, using her fists to part skin from muscle.

Finally she grabbed the loosened hide to her chest and used her body weight to pull the skin free. It hung down from the deer's forelegs. With a few quick cuts she severed the last connection between skin and animal. She sprinkled the hide with salt and left it for the tanners.

Her part was done. She removed her hunting robe and hung it on a hook. The rough wool reeked of stale sweat, blood, and dirt; the fabric was so stiff with lanolin that it might almost stand up on its own. Her gray woolen underdress was dry, though. She plunged her hands into a bucket of water and scrubbed her skin with a bar of lye soap. She waved her arms to shake off the drops of water and pulled on the village robe that she had placed in the shed before she'd gone out to hunt.

She knew that Vered was expecting her to return, but she suddenly felt too tired to sit upright on the kitchen stool. She'd rest here for a minute, just to catch her breath. She curled up on the floor and tucked her hands under her face. In a few moments, she was asleep.

Chapter Eight

T he mountain loomed over them, its twin-peaked summit lost in the clouds. MrsKeller gazed upward, slack-jawed and speechless.

Lance wiped the sweat from his eyes. "Now I understand why it took us hours to get here. We weren't close to a small mountain range—we were far from an enormous one."

MrsKeller groaned. "We still have to climb it."

"Want to rest a minute?"

"Dude, are you kidding? I'm about to die here." MrsKeller's leather knapsack hit the ground with a thud, followed by MrsKeller.

The pack was a simple pouch with an overhanging flap, secured with a tightly knotted rope. MrsKeller leaned against it wearily, but he didn't seem to find it comfortable. He sat up again and eyed the knot with distaste.

"That's making a hole in my back," he said, and started to tug at the rope. The knot refused to yield, so he unsheathed his dagger. "If I had a little hobgoblin strength here"—he slashed downward—"I wouldn't have to do *this*."

The knot broke apart, and MrsKeller took a moment to admire his handiwork. "Now we'll see what's inside."

Lance moved in to get a better view.

MrsKeller raised the flap slowly. "It's heavy as a dead orc, I can tell you that."

A gust of wind ripped the leather from his hands and flung the pack open. MrsKeller's yelp of surprise quickly turned to laughter as he was completely enveloped in a cloud of feathers.

"No wonder you're so tired," Lance said. "You must have been carrying *thousands* of them."

MrsKeller stopped laughing. "Whatever I'm carrying, it's more than you are, I guarantee. Your pack looks almost empty."

"No it isn't." Lance unknotted his pack easily and reached inside. "Look at this." He pulled out a yard of rough brown cloth.

MrsKeller held a corner to his nose, gave it a quick sniff, then let it fall. "Smells like wool, and I feel itchy just looking at it."

Lance held the cloth to the sun. Lumps of dirt and small burrs were tangled in the fabric; it was definitely a woven blanket. Lance saw a crosshatch of light shining between the warp and weft. "Whoever made this didn't bother to get all the junk out of the wool," he said. "It looks kind of primitive."

"True," said MrsKeller. "But at least we know that somewhere—maybe just over the mountain—we're going to find some ordinary-type creatures, not to mention people who know how to weave."

Lance ran his fingers over the rough cloth. "I'm not so sure we'll find people like us, though. Maybe they'll be cavemen or something."

"Or maybe they're really advanced, except for this one guy

who's just bad at weaving." MrsKeller gave the pack a nudge. "What else have you got?"

Lance dropped the cloth and delved into the pack. His fingers closed on a suede water skin, which he held aloft to show MrsKeller. With his other hand he drew out a soft drawstring bag. The contents jingled.

MrsKeller's eyes widened. "Is that a money purse?"

"Feels like it." Lance untied the silken cord and poured a stream of plain round disks on the ground.

"Whoa." MrsKeller began to count the coins and sort them into piles. "Thirty coppers, twenty-five silvers, and my favorite"—he picked up a gleaming yellow disk—"two pieces of gold." He swept the coins into the purse and returned it to Lance. "Now I've gotta see if I have some."

MrsKeller reached into his own pack and pulled out a drawstring bag that was ten times larger than Lance's. In one swift motion he opened the bag and dumped out a clattering mass of small white shells.

He snatched one from the pile and examined it hopefully. Then his shoulders sagged and he hurled it into the desert. "Can you believe it? For a minute I thought we were rich."

He reached down for another, but Lance grabbed his arm. "Are you crazy? You can't just throw them out. They could be valuable."

"No way," MrsKeller said. "This represents ten pounds of trash loot—the kind of stuff that a vendor would buy for twenty-five coppers."

"But that's just in the game." Lance began to scoop the shells back into the bag to prevent MrsKeller from throwing more away. "It might be completely different here."

"Believe me, it's junk—like this." He pulled out a withered brown object with two dangling arms. "Ack." He dropped it quickly. "You know what that was, don't you?" Without waiting for an answer, MrsKeller kicked it away. "Vampire Batling."

"Maybe you'll *need* a Batling." Lance scrambled after it and returned it to the pack.

"Oh, sure. At two coppers a piece from the vendor? No one needs a Batling. Or this either." He retrieved a feather that had escaped the wind. "It's a Fell Hawk Feather: seven coppers for a stack of twenty-five."

He turned the whole pack upside down, naming the objects as they tumbled out. "Level 4 Sumalian Helm, level 7 Blunt-edged Throwing Knife. Sack of Slug Salt." He picked up a small leather purse and shook it next to his ear. "And here at last is my money purse." He counted the coins. "Kind of pitiful that I'm only carrying thirty silver. Should have gone to a vendor first."

Lance restuffed MrsKeller's pack with everything he could get his hands on, while MrsKeller's attention was drawn to the last item in his bag. He whistled with astonishment and held it up reverently.

"I don't get it," Lance said. "It looks like a moldy football."

"Don't you recognize Genuine Moldy Aged Gruyere? It's a fantastic potion—gives a +35 boost to speed for sixty minutes." MrsKeller placed it carefully on the ground and sighed with pleasure. "Now *that's* a great drop. Unfortunately, that's all I have. Let's see the rest of your stuff."

Lance rummaged in his pack and pulled out an elaborate

white shirt with puffy bell-shaped sleeves. "Check it out, MrsK—a pirate shirt from the Shipwreck Ahoy! quest. And also these." He held up a crudely tailored pair of brown, drawstring pants. "Level 5 Tattered Trousers, dropped by a Raging Bull."

The clothing was tailored to accommodate someone three times MrsKeller's girth, but Lance wadded both pieces into a hefty ball and tossed them at MrsKeller's bare chest. "These are clearly for you, missus. Not exactly your size, but you'll probably grow into them."

"If I grow up to be an orc . . ." MrsKeller had disappeared into the shirt, and his words were muffled until his head emerged through the neck hole. He looked down at himself and laughed. "I feel like I'm wearing a pup tent."

"Excellent," Lance said. "Room for a friend."

"Seriously—it's just what I need. Can't be going around in my toon's robe and letting all these folks see my boxers. What if they only wear briefs here? People would laugh. But are you sure you want to give these up?" MrsKeller said. "Next to me, you're going to look pretty sad in that plain brown tunic and those raggedy breeches."

Lance tried not to laugh as MrsKeller secured the excess fabric with his belt. "I'll deal with it," he said. "Now you just need one more thing, and your outfit will be complete."

He pulled out the bolt of wool and tossed it over MrsKeller's shoulders. "Voilà! Instant cloak."

MrsKeller wrapped it tightly around himself. "That's much better. But don't you want it?"

Lance waved a corner of his cloak. "This is fine—I'm plenty warm for now, and I have two more bolts of wool."

"How's your footwear?" MrsKeller tugged off a thick felted boot and revolved it slowly in his hands.

"Fine, I guess." Lance surveyed the clumsy-looking knee-length boots and wiggled his toes. "I'm surprised how well they fit."

MrsKeller frowned slightly. "Mine too. Everything else was tiny, though."

"What about your belt?" Lance said. "That fits."

MrsKeller ran his hands over the leather. "I guess it does, but I wish I had better weapons on it." He unsheathed the dagger and tested the edge with a professional air. "Not too sharp, unfortunately."

"Maybe I have something in this. It's the last thing in my pack." He pulled out a bulky crate made from thin slats of wood. The weight inside shifted. There were scratching sounds too, as if something alive in there was desperate to get out.

A waffling, hairy blob thrust itself out between two of the slats. It twitched compulsively, withdrew, then reappeared in another place where the slats were wider. This time a bit of white fur was visible, and a few long, brown hairs.

"Your critter!" MrsKeller exclaimed. "Got to be!"

With no hesitation now, Lance pried open the crate. Out hopped a brown-and-white lop-eared rabbit. It settled in the shade created by Lance's shadow and thrust a hind foot deep into one of its floppy ears. After a good scratch, it stretched out on its side and gazed at Lance calmly, with an unblinking eye.

Lance reached down and held the plump creature in his

arms. He could hardly believe that this was his noncombat pet. It was alive—truly alive.

The rabbit's heart was beating, and the feeling of life beneath his fingers made Lance's stomach growl. He saw himself sprawling on the cavern floor, face pressed into a corpse, feasting on the fresh blood. He could feel pure energy dripping down his throat, and in spite of himself, he licked his lips. Never had he yearned for anything as much. It was as though someone had given him a drug—crack or crystal meth—and he had decided to try it "just once," even though after one taste, he'd never be the same. He'd have to have more.

A slight breeze ruffled his hair, and he realized that sweat was pouring out of him. His clothes were soaked, and he was panting though clenched teeth. He opened his mouth and took a few deep breaths. The air was dry and dusty, but it was still air, and he needed it to live just as much as the rabbit did. He hadn't gone to the other side yet—he was still Lance: human, not zombie.

MrsKeller eyed him uneasily. "You feeling okay?"

"Sure," Lance said, trying to sound as if he meant it. "Just a bit of a shock, seeing the critter. Think it's soul-bound, for real?"

MrsKeller shrugged. "Let's see if it'll follow you up the mountain. I want to check out the view from the top."

"Me too. Maybe we'll see some familiar landmarks or something," Lance said.

"Absolutely." MrsKeller picked up the cheese. "But let's have a snack first."

"Are you kidding? We'll get salmonella or something."

"Salmonella?" MrsKeller laughed. "From Genuine Moldy

Aged Gruyere? It's a *health* potion, remember? It gives +35 to speed."

"In the game it does," Lance said. "Why are you so sure that it's a health potion here? Remember what TheGreatOne said? This place isn't identical to the game."

"But TheGreatOne's potion *did* work—woke me up right away. Why not this?" MrsKeller broke off a piece of cheese and held it out to Lance. "Go on. *Bon appétit.*"

"No way. It smells like puke."

"Be a man."

Lance pushed MrsKeller's hand aside. "You mean, be a guinea pig."

MrsKeller shrugged. "After me, then." He tossed the cheese into his mouth and choked it down. "Delicious. And now—" He slammed the cheese into Lance's mouth and got him into a headlock.

"Get off!" Lance said through his teeth.

"I'm on the varsity wrestling team. Last year I ranked second in the state, in the lightweight division," MrsKeller said. "Believe it, I can hang on a long, long time."

Lance forced himself to swallow. MrsKeller released the hold. "Good, right?"

Lance gave him a menacing smile. "You are dead meat."

"You think?" MrsKeller crouched down like a sprinter in the blocks. "You'll have to catch me first."

"No problem." Lance tried to grasp MrsKeller's cloak but lost his balance on the loose stones. The ground skittered away and he slid six feet down the mountain, pelted by a hail of tumbling rock. The rabbit stayed at his side, neatly avoiding the debris, and waited patiently for Lance to get to his feet.

Lance glared at the retreating form of MrsKeller. He made his hands into a megaphone and shouted, "I *own* you, MrsK."

The sound of MrsKeller's laughter was getting fainter. Lance pounded up the slope behind him. The pack jostled heavily against his back, and his breath was labored, but the rabbit was hopping as effortlessly as before. MrsKeller turned around and waved. Lance wanted to curse at him, but he had no breath to spare.

Then he gasped as if doused in icy water. A shock of glorious energy tore through his body. He started to run.

Chapter Nine

Rayva woke up abruptly when she heard the whispers. Where was she? She was cold and cramped from sleeping on the dirt floor, and there was a scent of iron and earth in her nostrils. She strained her eyes to see through the darkness. The shadows were playing tricks on her, taking the form of a body suspended on a rope. She got up, walked toward it cautiously, and touched the congealed slickness of raw meat. She clapped a hand over her mouth to stifle a scream, then realized where she was. She had fallen asleep in the shed, and the voices that woke her belonged to her keepers, Arabis and Sal.

She shrank back into a corner and hid behind her hunting robe. She could still hear them talking, but the words were muffled now.

"Hear me, Arabis. Our survival may depend on knowing the truth, and sending Aster is the easiest way."

"What if she's questioned by the Warriors?"

"Why would they question her? She's visited your sister before. . . ."

Rayva heard retreating footsteps, and the voices faded. The keepers must be headed for home. There'd be trouble if they caught her here, so she allowed them a thirty second lead before following.

With the utmost caution she slipped out of the shed and into the sharp night air. The wind tugged at her dress; she pulled the loose folds tightly around her and bent low to make herself as small as possible. Every impulse urged her to run, but she had to be stealthy.

She took small, flat-footed steps, which seemed to double the distance between shed and henhouse, where she and Vered slept. Arabis had just added six more hens to their already crowded hut. The high-strung exotics practically squawked their heads off whenever they were alarmed, so she'd have to open the latch and slip inside without making a sound.

Everything was made difficult because her hands were clumsy with cold, but she managed to reach her straw-stuffed mattress without waking the sleeping birds. Her dark gray cloak was folded neatly at the foot of the pallet, where she had left it that morning. She pulled it over her head and hugged her knees, trying to get warm.

"Psst."

Rayva started and turned toward the corner of the room where Vered slept. She put a finger to her lips, then realized that it was too dark for Vered to see her. She ran over to Vered's pallet and gently touched her arm.

"Not so loud." Rayva's voice was barely audible.

Vered sat up and leaned toward her. "Where have you been, child? I've been sick with worry."

"Fell asleep in the shed. Lucky for me that Sal and Arabis passed by. Woke me up."

"Late for them to be out," Vered said. "Something's up for sure."

"They were having an argument. I only caught a few things: They're sending Aster to Rhelle to find out about the monsters. And they're worried about the Warriors."

Vered interrupted with a joyous cry. "Praise the day! Mark my words, Rayva. If they're worried about the Warriors, they've got treason on their minds."

"Quiet, Vered, please! You'll wake the chickens." Rayva was surprised to hear how vicious Vered sounded. "Anyway, you're jumping to conclusions. Why would they care about the Warriors? Seyre is a Perdition village."

"Yes, yes!" Vered gripped one of Rayva's hands, almost crushing her fingers. "But are they as loyal as they were? I see cracks forming on the surface. Times are changing!"

Rayva shook her head doubtfully. "I wish I could believe that times would change for us." She got to her feet, suddenly aware of her sore muscles and the damp night air.

"Don't lose hope," Vered said. "Anything is possible. Remember Gert."

Rayva didn't respond to this. Gert was famous among the slaves because one morning she simply disappeared. Had she discovered a way to evade the boundary magic? Had she been taken away in secret? No one ever knew.

Unlike Vered, Rayva wasn't encouraged by the story. She'd feel hopeful if she could find out *how* to escape, but that continued to elude her. With a sigh she crept to her pallet, curled up beneath her cloak, and fell asleep.

* * *

It felt like she had barely closed her eyes when the cloak was ripped away. Without thinking, she made a grab for it. Her head collided with something hard, and she heard an angry yelp.

"Look what you've done!" Arabis swiped a trickle of blood from her lip. "Out of bed this instant."

Rayva hastily obeyed and darted a quick look at the furious woman. The keeper had left off her nightcap, showing her normally careful arrangement of curls tangled and unkempt.

Rayva stammered, "I didn't realize—"

"Hold your tongue and listen carefully to what I have to say." The keeper unfolded a square of suede and held up a bracelet. "Do you remember this?"

Rayva nodded and felt her stomach turn over. The traveling device! It was imbued with boundary magic that forced the slave to stay within twenty feet of the wearer. The Warriors had given it to Arabis when she had taken Rayva to Seyre. She hadn't seen it since.

Arabis continued, "My daughter and two others must go to Rhelle tomorrow. You will accompany her and attend to her needs. Needless to say, you'll be bound to her until you return."

Rayva wondered if she were dreaming. She wanted to hear Arabis repeat these words, so she asked, "I'm leaving the village?"

"Isn't that what I just said? The boys will come at dawn; be ready to follow them. Take your bow and arrows. I'll pack Aster's clothing. Vered will manage the food, and you will complete the other arrangements. If you begin now, there should be sufficient time."

Rayva turned to the other slave as soon as Arabis was gone. "You heard everything?"

"Every word," Vered said. "Quickly, come with me."

Rayva followed her into the kitchen. The old slave pushed aside a large jar of oil. Beneath it was a small hole in the earthen floor. Vered reached in carefully and pulled out a short thin knife, shaped like a needle.

"What's it for?" Rayva was sure it wasn't a kitchen tool.

"It's a stiletto," Vered said in a rapid whisper. "See the point? It can pierce chain mail and padded leather faster than winking." She slipped it back into a tube of leather and held the handle toward Rayva. "Strap it to your calf and keep your boots on. No one will know you're carrying it." Without waiting for Rayva's consent, she bent down and started to adjust the ties.

"What are you doing?" Rayva said in a horrified tone. "I can't use that. It's a murder weapon."

"Exactly. Use it, Rayva. You'll be away from the village, and there should be many opportunities to get the girl alone and take the bracelet. As long as you carry it, you can go wherever you want."

"You want me to kill Aster?" Rayva looked at the older slave as if she had never seen her before. "How can you say such a thing?"

"Easily. And I'd do it, too, if it would ensure my freedom."

"You keep it, then." Rayva tugged at the straps, but Vered's knots were surprisingly tight.

"I'll never have such an opportunity, Rayva." Vered's face

shone with a fierce joy. "I want you to have it."

Rayva felt the weight of the hidden blade against her skin and was suddenly overwhelmed with fear. "I can't—"

Rapid footsteps approached, and Arabis walked in. The conversation was over.

cɹɑpteɹ teɴ

Rayva stood alone outside the henhouse, waiting for the others. The only things stirring were the chickens, who pecked at the desiccated earth as if expecting to find treasure. Usually she was kind to the dimwitted fowls, but this morning she hardly noticed them. She could only glance back and forth between the front door of the cottage and the village road beyond.

She wondered for the twentieth time if something had gone wrong with the plans, when at last she saw the villagers ambling toward the house. She recognized the outlines of Strachys and Sorrel, two of the young men who supervised the tannery slaves.

Strachys was well built and not bad looking, but he was also conceited, nasty, and not very bright: he'd make a perfect husband for Aster. Sorrel was almost as bad, though not quite as self-satisfied as his friend. Sorrel had been born with a harelip, and though it was partially hidden under a wild beard and mustache, the girls overlooked him, and he was never treated with as much respect as the other young men.

They walked past Rayva without a word, though they had

plenty to say to Aster when she stepped outside to greet them. She was showing off her ridiculous new hairstyle: a "tower," so-called because the hair was wound around a felt cone to form a pillar on the crown of the head. Rayva thought it resembled a beehive rather than a tower; perhaps a homeless swarm would think so too.

The keepers came out to say good-bye. Arabis had never looked so haggard, even at this hour of the morning, which was never her best time. The bags under her eyes were swollen purple, and her smile was forced and unnatural. Sal displayed the same uneasiness. He had forgotten to comb down his fringe of hair, and his jowly face was as puffy as over-risen dough. Still, his good-byes were loud and jovial. The keepers wished the young men an easy journey, embraced their daughter, and gave Rayva two extra water skins to carry.

The three villagers walked together, and Rayva walked behind them, stooping under her heavy pack. She turned around and caught Vered's eye. The slaves exchanged a significant look, and Vered returned to the kitchen.

As they walked through the all-too-familiar district of Seyre, Rayva kept her eyes fixed on the gauzy pink fabric of Aster's long tunic. It clashed horribly with her red hair, but pink was the most expensive dye, so Aster considered it the best. Rayva felt sure the dress would look better on her, but slaves were not allowed to wear anything but brown, black, or gray.

The edge of the northern field marked the end of Seyre. A golden brown meadow of high grass lay ahead of them. Aster stepped onto the path that traversed it. Rayva followed close as a shadow. She eased herself over the boundary and held her breath, expecting to feel the collar's bite. Nothing happened. The collar was inert and heavy around her neck.

Tears welled up in her eyes. She blinked them away quickly. She didn't want to miss a single detail.

Rayva savored every moment of a journey that the others found completely unremarkable. They walked through the flat-bottomed valley on a well-trampled path that ran parallel to the river. The wind blew strongly through the dried prairie grasses, and the rustling sound mingled pleasantly with rushing water. The farther they were from the district, the clearer the water became. It flowed swiftly and seemed almost merry, as if happy to have cast off its sickness.

The valley should have been healthier as the water improved, but for long stretches the earth looked blighted. The meadow was choked with stinging nettles and thornbushes. Eventually even those coarse plants grew sparsely, then disappeared altogether. The loamy soil hardened and degenerated into loose stones and rubble.

Aster complained that she felt every pebble through her thin boots, and disapproved of the scenery. "Dreary, ugly, and the path is in a dreadful state."

"My brother said that half of Narduk went barren last month." Sorrel stopped to grab a handful of earth. He showed it to Strachys. "Maybe it's happening here, too."

Strachys was not impressed. "The farmers are only happy when there's a dozen things to complain about. This so-called barren soil? It was a dry autumn, and a hot summer." He gave Sorrel's hand a tap and sent the soil flying. "Depend on it: all will be well after one good rain."

"My brother is no alarmist. He thinks this is a real danger. The crops could fail. There'd be no feed for the animals—or for us."

Aster kicked a pebble petulantly. "It's certainly a danger for travelers. These paths should never have been allowed to get into such a state. It's a disgrace."

"And who will fix them?" Strachys said in a teasing voice. "Do you intend to take charge?"

"Don't be absurd." Aster waved her hand airily. "King Lair is in charge of all the building projects. No doubt he will see to this road once he's done with more important things."

"Like building your house," Strachys said.

Aster laughed heartily at this. "Exactly right. My house ought to come first."

Eventually, the path became smoother, and Aster's mood improved in proportion. As the morning eased into midday, she whiled away the time laughing and flirting with Strachys, and even with Sorrel. None of them acknowledged Rayva except when they wanted something from the pack.

Rayva was content to be left alone. She was completely absorbed with the new scenery and the strange desolate air that hung over the river valley. Her back was drenched with sweat, but she wasn't tired. She was accustomed to walking long distances while carrying heavy loads, and could have outstripped them all—even the young men, who were marching along at a good clip.

By late afternoon, though, Aster was finding it increasingly difficult to keep up. The young men had walked ahead, eager to reach the villages. Aster made an effort at first, but she was plump and unused to exertion. At home, when she wasn't busy with her clothes or hair, she spent her time beneath a shady tree, sewing or working a hand loom, but often doing nothing at all.

Walking over rough ground was something she never did, and without the young men to distract her, she was miserable. Her face was red and overheated, her hair was listing to one side, and she complained about the insects. Rayva couldn't see any, but Aster insisted she was being persecuted and swatted at one with a broad, dramatic gesture that upset her balance. She fell heavily, with one foot trapped between two stones.

Rayva bent down to free the imprisoned foot. Aster only howled with pain, certain that it was broken. She called for Strachys and Sorrel, but they were out of earshot.

"Run and fetch them, girl," she told Rayva. "Move it."

Rayva ran fast, knowing Aster was watching her. "Strachys, Sorrel . . ."

"Where's your mistress?" Sorrel asked.

Rayva gestured at the path. "Back there. She's hurt."

The young men rushed off nearly before she'd gotten the words out. Rayva followed, breathless with excitement. She had been completely out of Aster's sight, yet there hadn't been a single twinge from the collar. Was it broken?

A surge of hope went through her, but she kept her expression blank. She didn't want to arouse suspicion, and it would be terrible if they caught her smiling at Aster's misfortune.

At the moment, all eyes were on Aster. The young men hovered nearby, waiting for Rayva to come back and assess the damage. It was not fitting for them to touch Aster, and even if they had, their clumsy hands wouldn't have told them much.

Rayva, however, was well versed in anatomy, and the young men silently acknowledged her expertise by standing to the side to watch.

She sat cross-legged on the ground and gently lifted Aster's leg onto her lap. She ran her fingers over the ankle. It was slightly swollen already; she couldn't tell if it was a simple sprain or something worse. Holding Aster's heel in her hand, Rayva pushed the foot forward and back, and from side to side.

"You're hurting me," Aster screamed, pushing Rayva away. "Stupid girl. I can barely move it. How will I walk?"

Rayva kept her eyes on the ground, sick with disappointment that their trip might be cut short. "I can't tell how severe the injury is. If you're in a lot of pain, walking may not be possible."

"Don't worry," Strachys said. "We'll have someone from the village fetch you on a donkey."

Aster's cheeks flushed red. "You'd leave me here alone?"

"You won't be alone," Sorrel said, avoiding her indignant eyes. "The slave can guard you perfectly well—not that you'll need it."

Aster shook her head vehemently. "I can walk if you just let me lean on you a little—one on either side."

"But the pace will be too slow." Sorrel's voice was peevish. "We'll never get to Rhelle by sundown."

Aster slung her arm around Sorrel's shoulder and gestured for Strachys to get on the other side. "There now," she said. "That's not so bad, is it?"

Strachys and Sorrel exchanged resigned glances and started to walk forward with their hands around her waist.

"You see?" she said. "We'll get there in no time at all."

But the ground was rocky and sometimes steep. Aster leaned heavily on the young men, and progress was slow.

Strachys rubbed the sweat from his face with his sleeve. "It's getting dark. We'll be out here all night if we don't get help."

"Don't leave me alone." Aster was instantly thrown into a panic. "What if something happens while you fetch help?"

Sorrel turned to his friend. "She's right," he said in a low voice. "We shouldn't leave her."

Rayva couldn't help noticing that she didn't count as company. No one gave a thought to *her* safety.

Aster, however, was triumphant. "Now you're talking sense," she said. "You can't leave an injured girl. My parents would have a fit."

Chapter Eleven

L ance fixed his sights on MrsKeller, who was standing on the flat space between the twin peaks. In his peripheral vision, colors and shapes moved and merged and refused to come into focus until he stopped running.

When he reached the peak, MrsKeller shouted, "That was awesome!"

"I know," Lance said modestly. "And I'm not even out of breath."

MrsKeller pointed to the rabbit, who was shaking the sand from its fur. "I was talking about the critter. He sticks with you at any speed, and just watch—" he lifted the animal from the ground. It struggled to get away. When he put it back down, it ran straight to Lance and settled between his feet. "Now *that*," he said, "is what I call soul bound."

"I wonder if he stays in my pack until I summon him." Lance shrugged out of the straps and put the rabbit inside. He left the flap open. It made no attempt to leave—just like in the game.

"Weird, huh?" MrsKeller said. His voice sounded odd, and

Lance noticed that his eyes were red and glassy.

"You okay, MrsKeller—I mean—Adam?"

"Well, you know—" MrsKeller paused and cleared his throat a few times. "TheGreatOne, the wyvern, the Red Plateau, Saddleback, your critter—it was all scary as hell. Not the critter," he amended. "But it was still just like the game. Know what I mean?"

Lance nodded as if he did, but then confessed. "Not really. I was—am—completely terrified."

"I'm not trying to say I'm braver than you," MrsKeller said quickly. "Just more delusional."

"You're not—"

"Seriously Lance, in the back of my mind I've been thinking—no problem. If we get eaten or killed in an earthquake, we can always run back to our corpses and rez, or pay off the cemetery shade and key out. Funny, right?" He shook his head. "I even wondered if I could whisper my father for help."

"Your father?"

"Yeah." MrsKeller seemed somewhat embarrassed. "He plays for, like, fourteen hours a day since he lost his job. It's lunatic. But even if it were possible, he'd never see me. We're not even on the same server." MrsKeller stared at the eastern horizon. "Still, I had a feeling we were in the game somehow, and soon enough we'd figure out how to leave. Then we get up here and I don't see the game layout, and for the first time it hits me: we're not in Discordia."

"Wait a second, Adam." Lance closed his eyes and tried to imagine the view from Saddleback Mountain. "We're *not* in the game." He opened his eyes and looked at the landscape again.

"But maybe it's not as different as all that. If this were the game, we'd be looking at the Borders from here, right?"

MrsKeller nodded.

"That road at the bottom of the mountain seems to be in the right place, and maybe we've just been thrown off because we've only seen the Borders when it's covered in snow." Lance pointed to the evergreens. "Couldn't that be the Borders forest, where we did all those quests?"

MrsKeller studied the area for a few seconds. "I guess it's possible," he said slowly. "But we ought to see the river, and the town of Seyre on the other side."

"Maybe it's there, but we can't see it because the game map's scale is off—making it seem like everything's closer than it really is."

MrsKeller gave a start of excitement, "If you're right . . ." He trailed off. "Let's work this through. We got here through a portal, right? Reaper's Horde—"

"And TheGreatOne left through it," Lance said. "But—"

"I know," said MrsKeller. "It's not there now. But if there's one portal, there might be more, and if the layout follows the game, we might already know where the others are."

"Oh, I get it," Lance said, catching his excitement. "Castle Ruinos, Jewel Cavern, Ardep's Mine—"

"Exactly! And maybe there'll be portals that will take us back home."

"Adam, you are brilliant."

MrsKeller flashed a shy smile. "Assuming I'm right."

"It's *got* to be right." Lance tightened the straps of his pack. "Let's get down there and find out."

MrsKeller nodded, and they half ran, half slid their way to the foot of the mountain. At the bottom they saw a dirt road going east, which was seamed with wheel ruts and dotted with animal droppings. Immense trees had been planted on either side, though there wasn't a single leaf on the branches or on the ground. There was a rigid order about the place, like a formal garden where every plant was deliberately planned and placed, and an army of gardeners worked full-time to root out stragglers or weeds.

"Funny how quiet it is," Lance said.

"Everything's dead." MrsKeller craned his head upward and squinted at the branches. "Even these trees."

"But it's cold," Lance protested. He drew his cloak around him. "On this side of the mountain, it seems to be autumn. The fields *should* be empty, and the leaves are down—that's normal."

"Oh, yeah? And where are they now? Did someone vacuum everything up?"

Lance frowned and picked up a handful of gritty soil. It had a dusty smell and formed little pellets, like factory-extruded gerbil food. Just holding it made his skin feel dry. He threw it down quickly and brushed his hand against his tunic. "Maybe you're right, MrsK. I don't think anything could grow in this."

MrsKeller tugged on one of his dreadlocks. "There's something really creepy about this place. And as far as I'm concerned, the sooner we get to Seyre, the better."

They shared another bit of aged gruyere and raced into the wind, mile after desolate mile. Their lips were cracked and their eyes were raw and dry, but otherwise they were comfortable, and the exertion felt less arduous than walking. They could talk without effort, but the sameness of the scenery was oppressive, and their conversation was desultory.

Lance was sick of wondering when they would reach the forest. After an especially long silence, he tried a different topic.

"When TheGreatOne told me that you were MrsKeller, I could hardly believe it."

"Pretty funny, right?"

"Quite the surprise," Lance said dryly.

Adam caught his expression and did a quick double take. "You didn't think I was a girl, did you?"

"Well . . ." Lance was suddenly interested in the shape of a passing cloud.

"Oh, lord. You did, didn't you?"

"No comment."

"You really thought I was a girl!"

"What was I supposed to think MrsKeller? What guy would call himself that—and what guy would choose a female hobgoblin in the first place?"

"You're kidding me, right? Ninety-nine percent of female chars are dudes."

Lance looked thoughtful. "Really? I never heard that."

"Maybe that's not the exact number," MrsKeller conceded, "but it's definitely a lot. What's the big deal? Male and female toons are identical in every single way except for looks, and a lot of guys would rather be watching a hot chick running around. There's more viewer satisfaction."

"You're saying that MrsKeller is hot?"

"I don't know about that," MrsKeller said. "She looks like my third-grade teacher."

"Let me guess: her name was Mrs. Keller."

"She had the Doom Shriek ability down pat." MrsKeller made a reminiscent smile. "The woman scared the crap out of me."

"And now you've gotten even, huh? Fightin' MrsK?"

"*Bien sûr*—and a spitting image she is, too."

They joked about their toons for a while, but in the back of Lance's mind he had a nagging feeling that the Wasteland was more dangerous than the settled parts of the world. He was sure that in the game the Borders forest was much closer to the foot of the mountain.

"Doesn't mean anything," MrsKeller said when Lance brought it up. "One inch on the Discordia map might equal twenty miles here." He sounded confident, but his brow was creased with worry, and he shouted about three times louder than Lance when the green line of forest finally came into view.

It was the strangest forest Lance had ever seen. The evergreens had branches that grew all the way to the ground, and the trees were so thick and dense they formed a living wall. If it hadn't been for the tunnel that was carved through the trees, they would have been forced to run around the entire forest.

MrsKeller's eyes were fixed on the shadowy passageway ahead, but Lance was looking back toward the mountains. He heard hoofbeats in the distance. From the corner of his eye he saw something move.

"MrsK!" he said. "Someone on horseback."

MrsKeller turned and watched uneasily as a tall rider galloped toward them. Apprehension quickly gave way to alarm and then to outright panic. He grabbed Lance's arm, nearly wrenching it from its socket, and propelled him toward the woods.

"You crazy?" Lance tried to pull away. He was nervous about meeting a Discordian, too, but this was ridiculous.

MrsKeller refused to stop. "The horse has no head, Lance. No *head*."

"What do you mean—no head?" The rider was closer now, and Lance saw it clearly for the first time. It was an equine creature with a man's flayed torso rising from a horse's broad chest. Its face seemed human, though the features were shrouded in green vapor.

Without realizing it, Lance screamed, and he and MrsKeller raced forward, their pounding feet obscured by clouds of dust. They were practically flying now, but their pursuer was closing the distance between them.

It was only two lengths away when Lance and MrsKeller reached the tunnel through the forest. They ducked inside and kept running. The path was narrow and claustrophobic, and the air was heavy with pine sap. Broken branches tore at their clothing and whipped their faces. Every moment Lance expected to hear the dreaded thunder of hoofbeats and see the cloud of green vapor, and yet he saw nothing and heard nothing but their headlong flight.

Lance halted abruptly. "Safe, right?"

"Think so."

Lance squeezed MrsKeller's arm, then bent down and braced himself against his thighs. His lungs were burning, and his legs felt like rubber. When he was able to speak he said,

"It's gone, right?" He peered into the darkness. "Why'd it stop chasing us?"

"Tunnel too small. Couldn't squeeze through." MrsKeller said between heaving breaths. "Lucky. Damn lucky."

They straightened up and kept going, too tired to manage more than a jog, but too nervous to go slower until they entered a new section of the forest. The trees were widely spaced here, and there was a sunlit clearing. A clear stream burbled over rounded stones.

They followed the path to a grove of aspens, where they decided to rest in an inviting drift of yellow leaves. Lance tilted his face toward the sun and marveled at being alive. For a few minutes they lay there, stupefied and immobile, until MrsKeller broke the silence.

"I'm never going to move again. Don't try to make me."

"I'm not," Lance said. "It's way too much effort."

After a moment MrsKeller said, "Did we go through Reaper's Horde this morning? It feels like weeks ago."

"Years, maybe," Lance said.

"And I had a snow day—a real big storm. They were calling it the storm of the century."

"Us too." Lance propped himself up on one elbow. "You live in New York?"

"Fort Lee."

"New Jersey? You don't sound it."

"I'm *from* Morgan City," MrsKeller said. After a pause he added, "Louisiana. But we moved up north."

Something about MrsKeller's voice prompted Lance to say, "Not a big fan of the Garden State?"

MrsKeller got to his feet as if he wanted to move away from this topic. "You could say that." He stretched and looked into the clearing. "I'll be back in a second. Nature break."

Lance closed his eyes. He was just drifting into a nap when he heard a scream. He sprang to his feet and looked for his friend.

"MrsKeller? You all right?"

There was no answer. Lance headed toward the stream that cut through the clearing. He thought he saw a flash of white. Was it the pirate shirt?

"MrsKeller?"

"Keep away from the water!"

Lance pulled up short. MrsKeller was splashing in the shallows. Then he saw the creature, black and shiny as a slug, but long as a boa constrictor. It had twined itself around MrsKeller's torso, its head level with MrsKeller's. Two thin tentacles hovered delicately over his face. MrsKeller had worked an arm free, drawn his dagger, and was trying to plunge the tip into the creature's side. The blade turned and flew out of his hand.

It landed in the grass near Lance's feet. He snatched it up and gripped the handle, rushed to the stream and attacked with all his strength. The dagger clanged against the rigid hide. Once again, the blade turned, and the knife was hurled aside.

The creature reared up and stretched its mouth open. Its jaws were lined with little tubes that oozed yellow slime. MrsKeller was in a frenzy to get away, but he was gripped tight. "Lance, do something!"

Lance wrapped his arms around the creature's head, but it

was like gripping steel cables. MrsKeller's face was purple and swollen. "Slug salt! Can you reach the pack?"

Lance's hands were shaking hard, but he managed to find the heavy sack.

He pulled it out, ripped it open, and threw a handful of salt directly into the slug's slavering mouth. Instantly the creature loosened its grip. Lance grabbed another handful and tossed it on the slug's slimy hide.

For a split second nothing happened. Then in one astonishing movement, the creature's skin peeled away like a banana. At that moment, its body turned flaccid. The deadly grip loosened, and it dropped to the ground.

MrsKeller propped himself up on his hands and knees, trying to catch his breath. When he could talk he said, "Would have killed me, but you—"

"It was the slug salt that saved you—not me." Lance tied the bag with trembling fingers. "And to think that we nearly—"

MrsKeller stopped him. "I know. I nearly threw it out, didn't I? Sweet Jesus—" He managed to sit up, and began to run his hand over his neck. "I still feel half strangled—and so slimy." He bent over the stream and scrubbed vigorously. "Stay close with that slug salt—just in case. That was so disgusting." MrsKeller couldn't repress a shudder. "Really disgusting. I think I've been scarred for *life*."

When he had finished washing, they began to search for the knife. MrsKeller noticed the glint of metal and swooped down to retrieve it. "Got it," he said, holding it aloft. He made a fair imitation of the hobgoblin Doom Shriek—a high-pitched wail, annoying as a car alarm. "Take that, slug beast," he yelled. "Nobody messes with MrsK!"

Lance started to laugh and egged him on from the sideline. He called out, "From victim to avenger!" and MrsKeller threw himself on the corpse, sinking all his weight behind the dagger's point.

The blade exploded into the flesh and let loose a geyser of viscera. Lashes of black blood splattered Lance's face, and he felt a sudden rush of heat. He clawed at his cheeks, trying to scrape the blood to his lips. He needed more. *More.* He was poised over the body, ready to plunge into it.

MrsKeller saw him out of the corner of his eye and whirled around. "What the hell are you doing?" He was laughing, as if Lance was just fooling around, but he turned pale at the sight of Lance's face.

Lance almost snarled at him. "Leave me alone." His voice was low and menacing.

MrsKeller backed off. "You're scaring me, man."

Lance tried to speak, but the zombie within pushed him aside. It hungered for the fresh kill. The human creature inside its head wanted to deprive it of the kill, but the zombie fought for control of the body. The struggle was brief because the zombie was powerful. It compelled the legs to lurch toward the river—and the blood. Blood was life. It would make the zombie strong.

Another obstacle appeared: a living creature that hurled itself in the zombie's path. It was weak and stank of fear, and it would be easy for the zombie to claim its life. The fragile skull would crumble like an eggshell beneath the zombie's fingers.

The zombie grasped the creature's head. The eyes bulged—

too green, bright, alive—they hurt him. The zombie shrank back.

The living creature screamed, *"Lance, stop!"* and the sound echoed and amplified. It squeezed the zombie aside and forced it to grow smaller. The living creature shook the body violently, and gradually human Lance began to fill the mind again until it reclaimed the whole. The zombie was gone, and Lance fell to the earth like a stone.

chapter twelve

L ance could hardly recall what had happened next. He'd
lain senseless in the grass for ages, dimly aware
that MrsKeller had covered him with all their bolts of wool.
MrsKeller huddled next to him, asking him questions, but
Lance couldn't answer: he was too dazed and tired to speak.
He lay on the cold ground, not caring if he stayed there all
night. MrsKeller kept talking to him and trying to get him on
his feet, but Lance couldn't bear the thought of getting up. He
was about to tell MrsKeller that he should just go and not risk
his life by hanging around with him, when the wind changed.
An aggressive, noisome cloud seem to grab him by the throat,
and all of his self-pity vanished in an instant, replaced by the
desire for fresh air.

"Where's that coming from?" He looked around wildly,
expecting to see another monster.

MrsKeller took a few cautious steps to the east. "Over there,
I think."

Lance followed reluctantly, walking along the side of the
stream until it merged into a wider river. They approached the

riverbank, step by cautious step. The smell intensified.

"Murrisks?" MrsKeller whispered. "The poison breath?"

Lance stared at the brown greasy sludge that coated the water. It steamed a bit, as if giving off heat.

"It's pollution."

"You think so?" MrsKeller went almost to the water's edge and tried to peer into the fetid depths. "There's nothing like that in the game."

"Maybe life in real Discordia is worse than it looks in the game."

"That's pretty messed up." MrsKeller said. "Monsters are one thing, but *pollution*? I never imagined Discordians were as bad as that."

"Even our side?" Lance hadn't given it much thought. After meeting the GreatOne, he automatically assumed the worst. "I'm afraid that we might—" he broke off suddenly. Nearby, a woman cried out.

She was on the opposite bank of the river, being pursued by a flock of tiny, shaggy goats. Suddenly the woman drew herself up, whirled around, and flailed her arms as if determined to make a last stand. The animals took this as a sign to charge, and she tripped on the hem of her shapeless tunic. It might have been a bad fall if it hadn't been broken by one of the slower goats.

She grabbed it by the collar while the others went bounding and leaping toward the woods.

Lance and MrsKeller saw the goats coming, and stationed themselves at the foot of the bridge to catch them as they ran by.

"Got one," MrsKeller yelled. He held it firmly and made a

grab for another. It made an end run around him and ran smack into Lance. He managed to grab its collar, then he snagged another. MrsKeller snuck up on the third and caught it by the tail.

The animal gave an outraged bleat and bit him savagely on the thigh. MrsKeller yelped in pain but didn't let go. The animal tried to prong him with its tiny horns, but MrsKeller took advantage of the proximity by grabbing its collar. "Got ya, you nasty goat." He gave it a shake and dragged it across the bridge.

The woman looked on anxiously, uncertain if the strangers were benefactors or thieves. When she saw them stoop low over the animals and haul them back across the bridge, her eyes opened wide in amazement. One of the goats took advantage of her distraction and began eating the end of her white braid.

"Are these your goats, ma'am?" MrsKeller asked. He shoved them toward her without letting go.

She grabbed them by the scruff of the neck and growled, "These naughty, evil wretches? Not mine, though they're my responsibility when Rayva's out hunting."

She glared down at her captives. One had buried its nose in a tuft of dry jewel weed; the other was calmly chewing the end of her braid.

"The only thing I know about goats is how to stew them or mince their nasty, thieving hearts. Do you hear me, Gilda?" She aimed a kick at the animal's ribs, but it shied away gracefully. "You'll be the first to go." The goat appeared to take its imminent doom in stride.

MrsKeller interrupted the exchange by offering to help her take the goats to their stable. The woman looked up and really *saw* the boys. She glanced at MrsKeller's pirate shirt three or four times, as if she could scarcely believe her eyes.

When she spoke again, her tone was much more reserved. "Thank you, no. I need no help, and if you would kindly release the animals, I will bid you farewell."

MrsKeller hesitated. His goats were already pawing the ground, as if preparing to bolt. "They'll run away again if we let go. Can't we bring them to your stable for you?"

The woman eyed them suspiciously. "What's your business in these parts, anyway? Are you visiting someone in Seyre?"

"Just passing through," Lance said. "We're more interested in finding work in a large market town"—he hesitated and then hazarded— "or a city."

"Hmmm," the woman said. "Downriver are the twin towns of Rhelle and Narduk. They're not big as market towns go, but since they don't have slaves, there might be work." She took another glance at the pirate shirt and added in a doubtful tone, "Depending on what you're willing to do."

"Oh, we're not particular," MrsKeller said airily.

The woman appeared almost scandalized by this, and Lance hurriedly asked her another question. "You were saying, a city nearby?"

"Liander is the only city in these parts." She made a loud disapproving sniff as if to say that it was one more city than was wanted. "And it's more than a day's journey away, so I suggest that you keep on your path."

"Just what we plan to do, ma'am," MrsKeller said smoothly. "But I get the feeling that our path goes right by your stable."

The woman finally relented. "I'm sorry to seem ungracious,

but these are uncertain times, and to be seen talking with strangers may bring a good deal of trouble." She gestured toward the village. "The shortest way is through the tannery—"

MrsKeller interrupted. "A tannery! *That's* what stinks so much."

The woman nodded grimly. "The curse of Seyre."

"How can you stand it?" said MrsKeller.

"You get used to it after a while. When you have no choice."

She began to lead them along a path that ran parallel to the river. "It takes longer to the goat shed this way, but at least we won't be seen."

The boys were perfectly willing to do whatever she suggested, and neither of them regretted moving downstream from the tannery.

Lance's back was aching from stooping over the goats, but at least his animals were cooperative. MrsKeller's goats were balky and frequently stopped to plant their cloven feet and lock their knees. He tugged on their collars so hard that their necks were stretched out at full length, yet they still refused to budge.

"These goats are kind of nervous," he said. "Are there predators around?"

"None but me," the woman said with a grim smile.

"How about Wulvers? Got a lot of them?"

She wrinkled her brow. "Wolf first?"

"Wulvers." MrsKeller raised his voice in case she was deaf.

"Quiet, lad," she said sharply. "It's not the first wolf, nor even the second that concerns me. There are other things abroad, more frightening than any beast."

"I don't know about that," Mrs. Keller said, "considering we just saw a plague beast and a strangleworm—"

The woman went pale. "So near?"

"I'm afraid so," MrsKeller said. "The strangleworm was just over the bridge in that forest, and the plague beast was between Saddleback Mountain and that big evergreen forest."

The woman didn't speak until they reached a small wooden hut that was standing all on its own in a thicket of prairie grass. The door was open, and the woman unceremoniously pushed each animal inside and indicated that the boys do the same. When the goats were secure, she said brusquely, "I can't stay any longer. They'll notice I've been gone, and I haven't finished preparing the evening meal. You lads stay in the shed with the goats tonight. If I can, I'll come back with some food. Whatever happens, be on your way at first light."

The boys thanked her, and before she closed the door she added, "One more thing. If you see Rayva, warn her about the beasts."

"Who's Rayva?" Lance said.

Vered slapped her forehead. "Another slave, of course. My mind is half gone. Just look for two girls together, perhaps accompanied by two lads. Aster is a well-grown villager with a pile of red hair on the top of her head. The young men are ordinary villagers from this town. Rayva has black hair—in the single braid, of course—and she's prettier than a spring morning, though far too pale—almost white. She'll be carrying a large leather pack, plus a bow, arrows, and a hunting knife." She paused. "Send her my greetings—my name is Vered—and the warning."

"We'll be glad to, ma'am." MrsKeller said. "But shouldn't we tell the others?"

"Not a word to them, if you please. If others hear such talk, they may turn you over to the Warriors."

The boys echoed, "The Warriors of Perdition?"

"Who else?" she said disgustedly. "One final thing. Tell Rayva to use the gift I gave her before it's too late."

Chapter Thirteen

The last bits of daylight shone through the gaps in the wood, briefly illuminating the inside of the shed. It was crudely constructed, with rough plank walls and an earthen floor covered with hay and goat pellets. The underside of the thatched roof was home to a thousand caterpillars, which hung down on sticky threads. At least the boys weren't cold. Five goats—even small ones—produce a surprising amount of heat in a confined space, and as MrsKeller observed, it's even warmer if they take a liking to you. Four of them were draped over his legs, and the fattest one leaned heavily against his right side, with its head thrust under his armpit. Since MrsKeller's left side was against the wall, the smallest goat had to wander around for some minutes, unable to find a spot. It finally wedged itself over MrsKeller's feet. The position couldn't possibly be comfortable, yet the goat seemed content.

When all the goats were settled, the rabbit emerged from Lance's pack.

"At last," said MrsKeller. "You don't write, you don't call. I was beginning to think you didn't care anymore." The rabbit ignored him and turned to face Lance.

The door opened just wide enough to admit a cloth bundle. "I can't stay, in case they catch me walking about," the woman said, "but here's some food for you. Keep a sharp watch for Rayva, and don't forget to tell her that it was Vered who sent you." She closed the door without acknowledging their thanks.

MrsKeller put the food aside and parked himself in front of Lance. "Okay, Lance. The time has come." He took a deep breath. "What is going on with you?"

Lance avoided his eyes. "You know already."

"I really don't."

"Come on, MrsKeller, you saw what happened. I'm a zombie."

"Yeah?" MrsKeller tried to laugh. "I'm a hobgoblin."

"In the game—that's all. Here, you're normal. But I—" Lance struggled for composure. "Back in the cave, I ate a mara."

"Get out, Lance. You ate a raw mara?" MrsKeller tried to pass this off as a joke, but his smile merely stretched the corners of his mouth.

Lance said, "When I came out of the dungeon, my mouth and face were covered with blood and flesh. I ate a mara, and I loved it. I loved the taste, I loved the smell—I'm telling you. I'm a zombie."

"But you're not one now." MrsKeller spoke with confidence, but Lance noticed that he drew back a few inches. "And you didn't look like a zombie back there. You looked like you."

"Really?" Lance felt inordinately encouraged by this. It *had* to be a good thing if he had kept his old form; yet somehow he wasn't completely convinced. "Totally normal? You're sure?"

"Well"—MrsKeller pursed his lips—"what do you look like in Real Life? Slightly deranged?"

"Be serious, MrsK. I tried to attack you back there."

MrsKeller's smile dimmed. "Your eyes looked red for a second, but otherwise you looked like you."

"But as soon as I saw that blood, I felt like a zombie inside."

MrsKeller began to unwrap Vered's bundle. "And you don't now?"

Lance shook his head.

"So you think blood triggers the transformation?"

"Seems that way."

MrsKeller pulled out a leathery brown strip and held something under Lance's nose. "How about this?"

Lance caught a whiff of smoke, beef, salt, and garlic. "The smell! Take it away."

MrsKeller shrugged. "Smells like a Slim Jim to me. I love that stuff." He shoved it into his mouth and scrutinized Lance's face. "How do you feel?"

"Did she give us anything else?" Lance said faintly. "I have a feeling I should avoid meat."

"Good idea." MrsKeller reached for another strip of dried beef. "They say it's good for you." He peered into the bag and pulled out a handful of dried fruit and a round ship's biscuit. "There's plenty more in there, if you're hungry." He took a big bite of biscuit, choked, and grabbed the water skin. "Jeez, that's just about the driest thing I ever ate."

Lance nibbled his more cautiously, taking sips of water between bites. "Tastes all right, though."

MrsKeller passed him some fruit. "This is better—dried apricot, I think. She probably added it to counteract the other stuff."

Lance worked his way through some biscuits and a few handfuls of fruit.

MrsKeller shook his head. "Dude, you're gonna be regretting that in the morning, I guarantee it."

"Compared to what might happen if I eat the meat? I don't think so."

Outside, a sharp crack sounded, as if someone had stepped on a dry twig. Both boys flinched and craned their necks in the direction of the noise.

After a minute Lance whispered, "I don't hear footsteps, do you?"

"Uh-uh, but I tell you what—that doesn't make me feel a whole lot better."

They listened in tense silence, but the sound was not repeated. Then the door creaked open. A sliver of attenuated darkness glided in and hunkered down on the floor in front of them. "I'm back." The voice sounded like the crunch of dry leaves.

MrsKeller gulped. "Who are you?"

"Have you any idea how long it's taken me to find you?" The voice dropped the dry-leaves sound effect and became merely annoyed.

"GreatOne?" MrsKeller asked.

"Who else? I *said* I was having some zombie issues, but at the first sign of trouble, you run off and hide among the goats."

When Lance heard "zombie issues," his mouth went dry.

MrsKeller pushed the animals aside and stood up. "We're

supposed to hang around worrying about your 'zombie issues'?" His hands were balled into fists. "You walked through rock, babbling like a madman, and then left us to out there to deal with an earthquake, a wyvern, a plague beast—"

The zombie interrupted, "Excellent, excellent! You fought them?"

MrsKeller hedged. "Well . . ."

"I'm impressed," the zombie continued.

"Hate to disappoint you," MrsKeller said. "We didn't fight. We ran."

"Ah." The zombie's enthusiasm dimmed. "But you did escape, which bodes well."

Lance cut in. "Hold on," he said. "If there's any chance that you're going to cut out before you get to the point, I want to know what I'm supposed to do about *my* zombie issue?"

TheGreatOne was taken aback. "What would that be?"

"Have you ever cannibalized something?"

TheGreatOne's glowing eyes seemed to bore through Lance's head, reading his thoughts. "I've not had the pleasure."

"Pleasure?" Lance laughed bitterly.

"You're not joking?" TheGreatOne leaned closer. "You've actually done it?"

The boys exchanged an uneasy glance. The zombie's surprise seemed genuine, but it didn't make sense.

"You haven't?" Lance asked.

The zombie brushed this aside. "Our quest is more important than ever. Lance may not have a lot of time in this form, and I need you both to look human. The good folk here don't even know about zombies yet. Alchemia is still working on that project, and all I can say is that the woman is a klutz when it comes to sorcery. She really has no idea, and all her little attempts are lurching and oozing around on the Dark Weald Peninsula. That's where she keeps the wand she's developed for raising and *razing* the dead." TheGreatOne roared with laughter. "Don't you get it? Raze? She has to destroy the bad ones?"

Lance and MrsKeller listened in stony silence.

The zombie opened his jaw and let loose a gusty sigh. "Oh, never mind. I guess it's too much to expect a little enthusiasm about an adventure that is a zillion times more exciting than the game. This adventure is real, and I suggest we start our quest as expeditiously as possible. We wouldn't want Lance to alter for good."

MrsKeller circled his arms around a goat and looked at the zombie in disbelief. "Somehow, your quest isn't at the top of my priority list. *Our* quest is to get home."

The zombie shook his finger reprovingly. "Cooperation, MrsKeller, that's the key to a successful group. You help me with my quest, I help you with yours."

Lance quickly took a seat near his friend. "We'd better get the details, Adam," he said in a low voice. "What if it's the only way?"

TheGreatOne seemed to have heard this perfectly. "Now you're getting into the spirit," he said in an approving tone. "So, the quest. Your goal is to find and remove Alchemia's wand—that's your Primo, Lance. I call this wand Alchemia's Doom, because ultimately its power will be used against her."

"Alchemia, the sorcerer?" Lance's voice went up an octave. "The most powerful person on this planet?"

"So far," the zombie conceded. "I expect that will change soon."

MrsKeller looked at Lance and shook his head. "This is crazy. We don't have any power at all, and we're supposed to fight her?" He turned to the zombie. "We're not going anywhere but home."

"Mutual support, guildies, that's what it's all about. I'll . . . Oh lord, here we go again." The red light began to pulse in his eye sockets.

"Pay attention to every word," said the zombie, "while I still make sense. Go to Liander. Take the ferry to the Dark Weald. It leaves in the morning."

"How do we find it?" Lance asked in a panicky tone. "Like the game map?"

"Yes, yes. I'll try to be at Weald, at the meeting stone. If I run into trouble, I won't show up in person until later."

Lance felt cold with dread. Everything depended on TheGreatOne, yet it looked like the zombie had lost control again. "Later, when?" he demanded.

"*Listen.* Go through the kitchen door in back of Wealock Prison. The kitchen crew will be expecting you."

"How's that going to work?" said MrsKeller in a belligerent tone.

The zombie began to speak more quickly. "I'll use my powers. You'll see. They'll put you to work, but it's only for a day. I'll hide a cache of weapons under the stone sink—special ones for the job."

"Sink?" Lance asked. "What sink?"

"In the *kitchen*, Lance. It won't be difficult. All you have to do is go up to Alchemia's tower, and I'll be there to help you with the wand. After that you can go home." The zombie unfolded himself and rose to his feet. His eye sockets were like glowing coals, and his jaw worked up and down noiselessly.

After a few seconds he spoke again. "I plan to meet. Assist. Primo. Alchemia's Doom, I call it. It will be. Haste, careful. Bet. Reurel. One al . . ." The syllables became increasingly garbled.

He turned away from them, and the door swung open. For a moment they saw the skeletal figure clearly, and then it was gone.

Lance and MrsKeller spent most of the night talking and planning. It made sense to try the Dark Weald in any case; that's where the portals might be. Just before dawn MrsKeller fell into a light doze. He looked so peaceful that Lance guessed he was dreaming of home. It was a shame to wake him, but Vered had warned them to leave early.

He shook him gently. "Wake up, MrsK. Breakfast time."

MrsKeller muttered, "Two eggs over easy, bacon, white toast, coffee," and went back to sleep.

Lance shook a little harder. "Adam, we have to leave!"

MrsKeller propped his eyes open. "Why am I covered in goat?" He pushed the little animals away and stood up. The goats bleated mournfully.

Lance gave MrsKeller half of a ship's biscuit and tossed the other half in his own mouth. MrsKeller doled out a helping of cheese, handing Lance a furry corner. Lance eyed it suspiciously. The mold was thicker and more substantial than it had been earlier, and the green was overlaid with a web of black spores.

"I think it's gotten more aged."

"It's probably stronger, then." MrsKeller popped his own piece into his mouth and managed to swallow without much choking.

Lance tried to do the same, but in his haste he aspirated instead of swallowing and had a violent coughing fit. MrsKeller thumped him on the back.

"See, it's growing on you," MrsKeller said above the noise.

"That's what I'm worried about—" Then Lance felt the welcome surge of power. "Ready to run?"

MrsKeller swung on his pack and bounded outside. "Let's go."

The sun was higher now, but the sky was heavy and gray, as if unwilling to part with the night. The only living creature they saw was the rabbit, which was taking the lead, covering the distance with enormous leaps. Its ears flapped like flags in the wind.

"If I had lungs like this at home," MrsKeller said, "I'd be the state high school champion of track and field."

"You might be the world champion."

"Nah," MrsKeller said. "Thumper over there would be the world champion."

As they ran the day grew darker. Low storm clouds massed together, and the sky took on the sickly yellow color of a fading bruise. A thunderstorm was on its way.

The river was wider and deeper here, and towering cliffs threw shadows over the valley. MrsKeller was glad to see the dark water, because now it looked like the river in the game.

He threw a few mock punches at Lance's ribs. "Isn't this familiar? Any minute now we'll see the bridge. The towns of Rhelle and Narduk will be on opposite banks, and then we're off to the city."

Lance paused a moment and squinted into the distance. "Hate to say it, but I don't see any sign of the towns."

MrsKeller skipped a stone across the water.

"Don't do that," Lance said. "Didn't someone do that in The Hobbit and wake up a giant squid or something?"

"That's just a book," MrsKeller said. "There's nothing alive around here. Nothing. *Nada. Niente. Nyet*-thing."

Lance grabbed his arm. "Shhh. Hear that?"

A low mournful cry filled the air.

MrsKeller dropped into a wrestler's crouch and looked around warily. "Where's it coming from?"

Lance craned his neck and tried to see around a bend in the river. "Maybe it's just the wind. Or maybe—"

"Wind," MrsKeller said. "Definitely." The sound grew louder and swelled into a keening crescendo of wordless grief. MrsKeller gulped. "Or maybe it's a banshee."

Suddenly it seemed like a good idea to hide the rabbit. Lance scooped it up and briefly cradled it against his chest before settling it into the bottom of his pack. The rabbit gazed calmly into Lance's face until the pack was closed.

The howls and sobs grew louder, and the weather seemed to respond in kind. The sky turned dark gray, wind roiled the surface of the river, and water crashed against the banks like ocean waves.

The boys put their heads down and fought against the wind, keeping to the path that would lead them to Liander. At a bend in the river, they saw her—a tiny woman squatting near the roots of a skeletal tree that pointed to the sky like an accusing finger. The woman's feet were in the shallows, and she was rocking back and forth on her heels. Her long hair was the color of mist and hung loose around her shoulders. The ends floated in the water and tangled with her washing.

From the side she was beautiful, but when she turned to face them, she revealed eyes that were bloodred and raw from crying, and a single cavernous nostril in the middle of her face.

Lance and MrsKeller began to back away slowly.

"Don't move," she shrieked. "I warn you now!"

They froze as she hauled three robes from the water, frowning over each one, then peremptorily tossing them back in. "Few dare to visit the Little Washer of Sorrows."

MrsKeller breathed the word *banshee.*

"They say that if you hear me cry, you'll know I am washing your burial shroud." She patted the surface of the water, and in response the wind died down and the river settled back in its banks.

The boys exchanged panicky looks, and MrsKeller jerked his head back, indicating that they should flee south.

The banshee narrowed her eyes. "I said *don't* move. These shrouds are not yours; you've come for some other reason." She curled her mouth into a mad, crooked grin. "I know—you want to ask for my hand in marriage. The banshee *do* marry, though

I haven't done so for many years. Many centuries, perhaps."

As she spoke, a bubble of gray-green mucus glooped from her nostril, rolled over her lips, and collected on her chin. Lance waited with horrified anticipation for the drop to fall. He could easily believe that the banshee hadn't married for centuries. The shock was that she had married at all.

For a few seconds, the globule clung tenaciously to the banshee's chin, suspended on a string. Then gravity claimed it, and Lance managed to stammer, "We're much too young for marriage. Much, much too young."

The banshee winked a bloodshot eye. "Perhaps you wish to capture me, then. The ancient lore says that if you do, I will reveal the name of someone who will soon die, and then I must grant you three wishes."

"Oh no," Lance said quickly, "we'd hate to interrupt your work."

"Absolutely," said MrsKeller. "You look busy. We'll let you get back to it."

"Busy?" The banshee smiled bitterly. "I'm always busy. And you, perhaps, are wiser than you look. People never seem to realize that wishes are like burrs. They get tangled in the warp and weft of the universe, and things change. Not always for the better." She returned to her washing.

Suddenly she threw back her head and let loose another wail. "Oh, sad. Doomed, the poor souls."

As if in sympathy, the wind picked up and the river churned. A bolt of lightning split the sky in two, followed by a clap of thunder. It was so close that the boys ducked and jumped backward. At the same moment, a second bolt of lightning arched into the tree at the riverbank, which burst into flames, casting a demonic glow on the banshee's face. "The Little Washer is not consumed!" With an exultant cry she picked up a burning branch and raced toward them.

For a second the boys were too terrified to move. Then, without exchanging a word, they tore up the path and ran hell-for-leather into the north.

Chapter Fourteen

Strachys and Sorrel lounged against a tree and watched Rayva build a fire, replenish the water skins, and serve a simple meal of dried sausages and bread. She spread a deerskin on the ground for Aster and folded an extra cloak on top of it for her to use as a blanket. She knew that Aster would prefer to sleep closer to the boys and far away from the slave, but the boundary magic forced her to keep Rayva close. She ordered her to lay at her side—on the ground, of course, not on the deerskin—or better still, to sit up and keep watch.

It made little difference to Rayva. Sleep was impossible. She sat on the damp ground, feeling the outline of the stiletto in her boot. She debated the wisdom of testing the boundary magic. If it truly were broken, she'd have time to get away, but where would she go? She was too close to the villages, and they'd be sure to send search parties after her. She'd almost certainly be caught.

If she used the knife, she'd have a better chance. She could murder the Seyrens while they slept, and do it so quickly they'd never realize what was happening. Then she'd pull the bracelet from Aster's wrist and sneak away. If she escaped notice on the road, she could reach the Northern Lands. She would find a kind family who wanted a girl to do their chores, or hunt, or watch the children—anything and everything, as long as they were good to her and willing to give her a home. Or maybe she'd find druids who would teach her new ways to live in the forest and allow her to fight with them against the evil sorceress. Everyone would call her a valiant fighter, and know that she was dedicated to the cause of righteousness.

It was a worthy plan, but impossible. If she had to murder to buy her freedom, she'd be as wicked as the Perdition supporters, and as heartless as the Seyrens. If that was the cost of freedom, it was too much to pay.

She lay awake all night with a bitter taste in her mouth. At first light, all hope died and the faces of the sleeping Seyrens filled her with rage. They'd never know how close they had been to death.

Rayva had the fire ready and was preparing their breakfast, and she watched with half an eye as Aster tried to put some weight on her foot. She stood on one leg, bracing herself against a tree, with one hand grasping Sorrel's shoulder. Tentatively she touched the swollen foot to the ground and winced.

"Is it bad?" he asked.

Her face was drawn in pain. "Very. I don't think I can walk alone."

"Then you shouldn't try," Sorrel said. "We're not far from the village now, and we'll be back before you know it."

Aster was reluctant to let them go on without her, but after a few halfhearted protests, she agreed.

Rayva knew that Aster had only given in because she didn't want to appear in Rhelle with her hair in such a state. Half the tower had come down, and the whole thing was tangled with twigs and grass. Rayva knew they'd need every minute and more to repair the damage.

The young men were nearly packed when a hollow cry began to echo overhead.

Sorrel flinched at the sound. "What's *that*?"

"No idea." Strachys turned a slow circle, searching the sky. "Never heard anything like it."

In spite of her injury, Aster rose from the ground and held out her arms. "Get me out of here," she said in a hoarse whisper. "I'm not waiting around for that thing to attack."

The wailing increased. Aster grabbed Sorrel's sleeve and pulled him over, then slung her arm around Strachys. "Let's go!" she said, and the boys acquiesced by putting their arms around her waist.

The river valley had turned rocky and desolate again. Aster struggled over the stones. She kept her left knee bent, to prevent the foot from touching the ground, and hopped along on the right foot. In her anxiety to get to the town, she exerted herself much more than she had the day before, but still their progress was slow. The wailing had died away, but everyone remained wary and ill at ease. For some time the Seyrens only asked each other what could possibly make such a noise, but since no one could answer the question nor think of anything else to say, they just walked and watched.

Rayva kept pace behind them, and no one noticed how often she searched the landscape, trying to get a glimpse of whatever had made that noise. Rayva felt that she had finally found something that sounded as sad as she felt, and she wasn't frightened at all.

When the noise did not return, the Seyrens' mood began to lift. The land seemed healthier too: real soil now instead of rocks, and much evidence of useful human activity. The fields were cut into neat borders, and the upturned earth was rich and sweet-smelling. Pasture lands were carefully fenced to keep livestock out of the crops, and boundaries were defined by stone walls that had been constructed with considerable skill.

Most of the harvest had been brought in except for the hardier crops: cabbages, brussels sprouts, and turnips, which would reach their peak of flavor just before the frost. That would not be long in coming, Rayva guessed. The morning was well under way, but there was still a distinct nip to the air.

The young men paused to switch sides. Aster saw how tired they were. "We'll be there soon, don't you think?" she said. "These fields are just outside Rhelle."

Suddenly the cries began again, and Aster clutched the boys in panic. "It's back! Following us!"

Sorrel gave her hand a perfunctory pat. His fingers trembled. "I don't think we're in danger," Sorrel said. "It sounds sad, not aggressive."

Strachys turned impatiently. "Let's just get to the village."

"I don't think I can go on," Aster said. "My foot throbs and the pain is traveling all the way up my leg. And the other leg is so tired."

"Aster, you'll have to force yourself," Strachys said.

Aster only shook her head. "I can't."

Sorrel coaxed her on. "See that turning? When the road forks, we go to the right, and the village will be directly before us."

She took a staggering hop forward, and they inched toward the village.

Rayva's nose twitched. Fire. She looked for black smoke: perhaps a thatched roof had caught fire. Yet even as she suggested this to herself, she knew that whatever it was was worse than that. The smell was too thick and choking, and when they drew nearer, she could hardly believe what she saw.

The village was gone—nothing was left but charred stone and blackened bits of timber that rose from the ground like bare ribs. A few walls were still standing, but most had succumbed to the flames. The fire had taken the wooden crossbeams and thatched roofs, and whatever furniture there was had been consumed or perhaps carted away if anyone had had time to salvage their possessions. Wisps of smoke still rose from the ground, but nothing else moved as far as the eye could see.

First they could only stand and gape. But after the first wave of shock passed, Aster broke the silence.

"Only the Warriors could have done this."

"Don't speak of it," Sorrel said.

Aster turned her tear-stained face toward him. "Is it possible that our people escaped to Narduk? It's so close—just across the bridge."

Rayva saw the three Seyrens exchange looks of mutual horror. The same thought occurred to her as well. Was Narduk still standing?

Aster was now making a desperate effort to hurry forward, but it was difficult for her to maneuver through the streets. She stumbled frequently, and once knocked her good foot against a pile of debris. She drew back as the charred stone and timber rolled away, then pointed to something and screamed.

It was a human head on a severed neck, badly burned but still retaining a hank of hair, one blackened eye, and part of a nose with an iron ring through it.

Rayva shut her eyes and fought down a wave of nausea. She heard Sorrel urge Aster to keep going, that it was dangerous to stay.

The road leading to the river crossing was relatively clear, and they were able to move more quickly. Fear and anxiety increased their speed, but they had to stop short when they reached the riverbank. "The bridge is gone!" Aster said. Her voice rose with hysteria. "It couldn't have just disappeared—unless it was done by magic." She tore at her matted hair with one hand, almost ripping a clump from her head.

Once again they heard the keening cry. It sounded closer now. "She's calling our doom," Aster said in a hoarse whisper. "I know it."

"Don't listen," Sorrel said. "You just have to cross the river. Everything will be fine once we get across."

Aster whipped her tangled hair in his face. She was wild with terror, oblivious to her appearance.

Sorrel shook her and tried to make her hear him. "Aster, we don't need the bridge to get across. We'll help you, and the slave will stand guard on the other bank."

Strachys turned to Rayva. "You go first and see how deep it gets. Then ready your bow and arrow and prepare to defend your mistress." He reached into his pack and withdrew a nail-studded wooden ball affixed to an oak club by a strong chain.

Rayva waded in as quickly as she could, fighting to stay upright in the current. She held her weapons aloft to keep the bow string dry during the crossing. The icy water crept past her waist. Then the bottom of the river dropped lower suddenly, forcing her to tread water with her legs. As soon as she reached the other bank she began to string her bow with numb, clumsy fingers.

Aster shouted, "Did you see? The slave swims. I can't."

"We're with you," Sorrel said. "You're not alone."

"Too late." Aster's voice vibrated hysterically. "Hear that?"

There was the sound of something galloping toward them over stony ground.

Aster was frozen at the water's edge, eyes wide with fear. The hoofbeats grew louder. A hideous creature galloped toward them, part horse and part man. It had no skin to cover its muscles and veins, and its long sinewy arms extended toward them, twitching and pulsing.

Rayva dashed into the river to get a clear shot of the beast. She gripped her bow firmly and sent an arrow singing through the air. It pierced the creature's chest but passed through to the other side without doing a speck of damage. Her second arrow was just as useless. Before she could manage a third, the beast had its hands around Aster's neck. The young men pounded its flanks with mace and sword, but the beast flicked them away like horseflies. It lifted Aster off her feet and exhaled into her face before tossing her on the ground.

It grabbed the young men next and roared its poisonous

breath into their faces, too. Then it looked at Rayva, but made no attempt to catch her. Instead it wheeled around and ran back into the forest.

The three Seyrens were gasping for air. They hauled themselves to their hands and knees and crawled along the riverbank. The distant wailing began again in waves of shrieks and full-throated cries. Rayva saw Strachys kneel with his forehead against his knees, hands pressed to the ground. Aster and Sorrel had managed to get to their feet, and between the two of them, they pulled him upright.

"Rayva! Rayva dear," Aster called. She stretched out her arms and implored Rayva with her eyes.

"Help us," Sorrel said in a whisper.

Rayva looked at them with horror and pity, and shook her head. What could she do for them? What did Aster want from her? The three Seyrens were no better than plague beasts themselves now. She wouldn't go near them, no matter how much they begged.

Without a backward glance she raced toward the town, too shocked to realize she was free. She pounded on the first doorway she saw. There was no answer. In desperation she turned the handle. It gave way. She shouted for help, but before the first syllable left her mouth, she felt a tremendous blow at the back of her head, and all was dark.

Chapter Fifteen

L ance and Adam ran north in a blind frenzy, never daring to look back. Lance's only thought was to get away from the banshee. It never occurred to him that there might be other dangers, until out of the blue a man jumped into their path and threw them both to the ground.

He wore the uniform of a midlevel brigand: padded leather armor covered by chain mail. A thin chain around his neck held a silver whistle, and a thick leather belt held his weapons. Lance jumped to his feet, ready to fight, but the man caught him in a lasso and bound him tightly. Then he wrenched MrsKeller to his feet and pinned his arms behind his back. MrsKeller bellowed and twisted his body like a spring. In a motion too quick for Lance to follow, he broke the man's hold and faced him, poised for the next round.

Lance tried to back away, thinking of the rabbit laying low at the bottom of his pack. The brigand would claim it soon enough, but first he had to deal with MrsKeller.

The brigand gave MrsKeller an approving smile. "Very

nice—" MrsKeller cut him off by slamming his skull into the brigand's solar plexus.

For a moment the man was stunned. MrsKeller grappled for position, but in another moment the brigand recovered and, with astonishing speed, bound the boys back to back, with Lance's pack squashed between them. The rabbit kicked hard once and then went still.

Doesn't mean anything, Lance told himself. It's probably okay. Rabbits do fine in a little space. It'll curl up small.

The brigand watched them struggle with mild interest. "Enough, lads," he said finally. "Learn to recognize when you're beat. When Duncan Overbrook makes a knot, it's *tied*." He bent down and began to open a large leather pack.

"That's mine!" MrsKeller said.

"Is it?" The brigand began to sort through the contents. "I'd say not, and since I'm the one holding it, there can be no dispute." He held up the dagger and tested its blade with his thumb. "I never quite liked the balance of this knife." He threw it up in the air and caught it neatly by the handle. "On the other hand, an extra blade is an extra blade." He looked into the purse and smiled, though he was puzzled by the slug salt. "You must be planning—" He caught himself. "I'm a great one for pickles myself."

When he found the cheese, however, his eyes narrowed. "Could it be?" He carved off a tiny sliver and placed it reverently on his tongue. "The most precious of the druid's art, carried in a beggar's sack. Rewards beyond measure will be mine when I bring you to the Warriors."

He slung MrsKeller's pack over one shoulder and gave the

rope a sharp pull. "On your feet, traitors. We have a fair bit of walking to do."

MrsKeller murmured, "Poor bunny," and the brigand gave him a sharp look.

"What bunya?" he said with a gloating smile. "Have I caught a real druid?"

Lance felt like knocking the smirk off the man's face. He struggled against the tight bonds as the brigand looked on with amusement. Lance redoubled his efforts.

He remembered the strength he'd had after eating the mara and wished he had some now. He closed his eyes and thought about tearing through flesh and how good it had tasted, and the terrible craving that had overwhelmed him when he'd felt the strangleworm's blood running down his face.

He flailed against the rope, but his desperate efforts only made the knots tighter. Lance felt as if he were sliding down a steep slope, and every second he went faster and faster, making it impossible to stop until he reached the bottom.

Then the zombie looked out from his eyes, and the brigand's laughter seemed far away, muffled by Lance's rotting ears. His flesh withered rapidly. The ropes slacked, and he broke free with the smallest gesture.

The brigand moaned with terror, too frightened to call for help. He groped for the whistle around his neck, but his fingers trembled, and he needed both hands to raise the whistle to his lips. He sounded one short, high-pitched alarm as the zombie walked toward him.

"Demon!" cried the brigand, in a voice as high and shrill as a kettle whistle. He tottered—nearly fainting. "Don't come nearer. My people are on their way."

The brigand's eyes were fixed on the creature coming toward him. It wore the boy's clothing, and carried the boy's pack, but everything else had changed. Its face was bloated and sagging. Maggots appeared and feasted on the rotting skin. Soon the entire jaw was exposed. Then the brigand saw the sharpened teeth. With a shriek of terror, he broke through his paralysis and began to run.

The zombie ran after him, unaware of the small creature that had managed to squeeze out of the pack. It scrambled onto the zombie's shoulder. The zombie couldn't feel the scrape of its nails, but it felt the warmth of live food at hand. Saliva oozed from the zombie's mouth as it squeezed the little morsel, feeling the pounding heart and rapid pulse. The zombie lifted it toward his mouth. The rabbit cocked its head and gave the zombie a cross-eyed look.

"No, Lance, not the rabbit!"

The zombie heard a familiar voice, and Lance peered out from the zombie's eye sockets. The zombie turned, and Lance saw a distant image of his friend, as if he were viewing him through a concave window.

The rabbit's nose twitched. Lance could see it clearly now. He could even see the sun shining through its ears, revealing a tracery of fine veins. The rabbit's fur was soft against his skin, and the sensation reminded him of what it felt like to be completely whole and alive. Slowly he lowered the rabbit from his mouth and set him on the ground.

MrsKeller approached cautiously. "Skin. Coming back." He laid his hand on Lance's forehead as if checking for a fever.

Lance sat down and rested his forehead on his knees, drained of all emotion.

"You're okay now. You're okay."

Suddenly Lance was drenched in icy sweat. "Gonna be sick."

"Go on," MrsKeller said. "You'll feel better afterward." He patted Lance's back, and Lance remembered when he was little and his mother used to hold his head while he vomited into a bucket because the toilet was just too far away. Afterward she'd wipe his face with a warm washcloth and tuck him in. She always read him stories when he was well enough to listen, and then she'd tempt him with a little toast: thin slices of Pepperidge Farm white bread spread with the merest scraping of butter. He loved that toast.

Gradually the nausea receded and Lance lay on the ground with his eyes closed.

MrsKeller tucked his cloak around him. "Mm, mm, *mm*," he said. "You look like fifty kinds of bad."

Lance stared at his hands as though he didn't recognize them. "I was a corpse. A stinking corpse."

"It was the maggots in your eye sockets that got to *me*," MrsKeller said matter-of-factly.

Lance turned his hands over and stared at his palms. The rabbit took this as an invitation to climb up and get comfortable, but it was too plump to fit.

"Look at this guy." MrsKeller gave the rabbit an affectionate pat. "This here is a genuine, bind-on-pickup-therapy rabbit—very rare."

Lance drew in a shuddering breath and squeezed his eyes shut to keep the tears back. He concentrated on the reassuring sound of MrsKeller's voice as he spun a theory about the rabbit's special powers.

"Tell you what," MrsKeller said suddenly. "I think the bunny helped you get back to your real self, because he's soul-bound to your real self. He won't *allow* you to be a zombie for long."

Lance stroked the rabbit's ears. "I wish it were true."

MrsKeller shrugged. "Might be."

Lance shook his head. "You're giving him too much credit. Your voice seemed to bring me back. Maybe *you* have special powers."

"I don't know about that." MrsKeller flushed with embarrassment. "If you want to talk special powers, how about yours? You may be somewhat rotted, but the way you ran that brigand off was awesome."

Chapter Sixteen

hey didn't walk far before the first bit of thatched roof came into view. MrsKeller gave Lance a celebratory sock on the arm. "That's Narduk—I'd bet you any money."

Lance felt unsettled. The wind was carrying a strong scent of scorched timber and soot, but he couldn't see any smoke. "I smell fire, don't you?"

MrsKeller tilted his nose in the air. "For sure, but it smells like it's coming from Rhelle, not Narduk."

"Yeah, if these towns *are* Rhelle and Narduk." Lance's brow was creased with worry. "Anyway, it smells like something major."

They turned off the path and onto a dirt road. After a few minutes, they came to a small village situated around a pond and a fenced village green. Thatched cottages lined the road on either side, each with its own kitchen garden. The houses were tiny—none larger than a two-car garage.

MrsKeller waved his hand toward the nearest house as if it settled everything. "See? Everything's fine here. The fire must have been in Rhelle."

Lance made a slow revolution, trying to take it all in. Real people lived here, and their homes were nothing like the quaint dwellings in the game: no front steps, porches, lattice-paned windows, or stone chimneys. Their one advanced architectural feature was the tight bunches of thatch that covered the roofs.

"In the game, Narduk looks a lot more developed than this," Lance whispered. "There's a market square, a smithy, an inn—lots of shops, lots of people. This place looks deserted."

"Maybe they're out in the fields, or gone to a market day at another town." Lance edged past a sow and four piglets that were rooting through a pile of refuse. "Let's knock on one of these doors and find out where we are, okay?"

MrsKeller nodded and turned away just as the pigs began to feast on something gray and slimy. "Are those *guts*?" MrsKeller exclaimed. "Remind me never to eat pork again."

They walked to the next cottage. A chunk of whitewash had fallen away, revealing a basket weave of sticks and reeds coated with mud and manure. They could see only one window and a wide wooden door.

MrsKeller knocked. "Anyone home?"

There was no answer. MrsKeller slowly opened the door, and they both stepped inside. It took a minute for their eyes to adjust to the gloom. They were standing on an earthen floor covered with a thick layer of sweet-smelling reeds. In the center of the room was an open fireplace lined with smooth stones, but there was no chimney. Smoke must have filled the whole room when the fire was lit; though, as Lance pointed out, some must have seeped outside through the thatched roof.

"Drafty," Lance whispered. "I can feel the wind blowing through the walls."

"The animals probably don't mind," MrsKeller said in an equally low tone. "Wherever they are."

"Animals?" Lance said. "What are you talking about?"

"The ones who live here," said MrsKeller.

"It's not a *barn*."

"Yes it is," MrsKeller said. "Check it out."

Lance joined him at the far side of the room and MrsKeller gestured to an area that had been sectioned off by a low wall. There was a hay rack in the corner filled with a pile of straw, and a bucket half full of water.

"See what I mean," said Mrs. Keller.

Lance nodded. "But I think people lived here too."

"But the place doesn't look finished," MrsKeller said. "You think the people were just camping out?"

"No way. People have lived here for a long time: look at the soot on the walls. Don't tell me there weren't animals in the barn area. The evidence is unmistakable."

"True that," MrsKeller said. "Perhaps the family is at their summer home."

"Right," Lance said. "In the country."

They walked to the next house and saw a similar setup. The structure of the house was almost identical, but there were a few more signs of human habitation. A large black cooking pot was suspended by a chain over the fireplace, and there was a wide straw mattress in a corner of the room. MrsKeller gave it a kick, and a puff of dust rose in the air.

"Very comfy," he said. "And plenty of room for the whole family."

"Who seem to be missing."

The boys continued on to the next house, which was also vacant, as was the next and the next. The inhabitants were nowhere to be seen . . . except for one person lying on the ground, near a shed.

"You think he's dead?" MrsKeller asked in a low voice.

"God, I hope not."

As they got closer, Lance thought he could discern a curved line of the hip sloping down to a narrow waist: probably a female, curled into a ball and covered with a cloak and hood. She was holding the cloth tightly over her lower face so that Lance could only see a maggot-white forehead and two staring black eyes.

The girl stood up suddenly and reached for her scabbard. It was empty. She touched her back with one hand. "My pack!" she cried. "My weapons!" The girl braced herself against the door, then lurched into a run. The boys caught up to her easily.

"We didn't rob you," Lance said. "We want to help you."

Her legs wobbled, then nearly collapsed beneath her. She sat down and planted both palms flat on the ground to steady herself.

MrsKeller bent over her. "Are you all right?"

"Fine," she said, but her head hung down and her breath was shallow.

She looked anything but fine, Lance thought. Her clothing was soaking wet, and she seemed too weak to move. "You're hurt."

Instead of answering, she took off her hood and flipped her long braid over her chest. Her stark-white skin and black hair made her look like a pen-and-ink illustration from a book of fairy tales.

She touched the base of her head and winced. "Someone tried to crack my skull."

MrsKeller looked around warily. "Let's get her out of here," he whispered to Lance. "Help me lift her." He tried to hold one of her arms.

She snatched it away. "Don't you dare touch me."

MrsKeller blushed a dusky rose beneath his light-brown skin. "We're just trying to help."

"It's not safe," Lance added. "We can take you home if you tell us where you live."

"Home?" She dragged the back of her hand across her forehead. "Where's that? I don't even . . ."

"That's from being hit on the head," MrsKeller said sympathetically. "Once I had a concussion from falling out of a tree. Not fun."

"Do you live in one of these houses?" Lance asked.

She started violently and twisted around. "Where am I?"

"We're not sure." Lance said. "Maybe Narduk?"

An anguished cry burst from her lips. "Oh no!" She clapped her hands on either side of her face. The wind caught up a few locks of hair, and they writhed around her head like snakes.

"What's happened?" Lance asked.

"Burned. Destroyed—and worse. They're all dead!" Her voice thrummed with terror. "I can't stay here. It may come back. There may be others!"

"What may come back?" MrsKeller asked. "What others?"

The girl squeezed her eyes shut. "What have I done?"

MrsKeller edged closer. "Tell us what happened so we can help you."

She started speaking very fast. "A plague beast. We saw one. Near the riverbank. Rhelle side, not here. They sent me across to shoot it. It attacked. Them, not me. It didn't try to cross the water. I shot an arrow through it. It galloped away." Her dark brows contracted. "They begged me to help, but I ran away."

"What else could you have done?" Lance said. It was a real question. He wondered if there might be an antidote for the poison, since there was in the game. "If the plague beast attacked them, wouldn't they die anyway?"

She got to her feet and tottered unsteadily toward the path. She could only manage to take a few steps. The boys grasped her arms and helped her walk. She was too weak to protest, and allowed them to walk her through the town and back to the path by the river.

When they let go of her arms, she wandered away as if in a trance and splashed into the water, just over her knees. She stood still for a moment while she tugged on the metal band at her neck. Her nails turned even whiter as she pressed her fingers against the metal, but it didn't make the smallest bit of difference.

"Hey," MrsKeller said. "You're going to hurt yourself."

"Doesn't matter. I'm dead already. The Seyrens will come after me."

"Seyre?" Lance looked at MrsKeller. "She must be the one." He turned to the girl. "You must be Rayva."

She gasped but said nothing.

"A lady told us to find you," MrsKeller said. "Lady by the name of—" He paused. "Started with a V—"

"Vered," Lance said.

The girl covered her face and sobbed in an agony of grief. Her neck was bowed, revealing the wound. A slice of skin had been torn away, and it oozed blood. She was even paler than before, and covered in sweat. She leaned forward and retched. MrsKeller held her shoulders to keep her out of the water. "Lance—give me a hand—she's fainted."

Lance saw the blood and felt the zombie looking out, desperate to reach into the wound and to tear the neck open. He forced himself to turn away, then noticed someone watching him from the riverbank. It was Duncan, the brigand who had stolen MrsKeller's pack, and maybe Rayva's too. Had he returned for Lance's? He had nothing of value—only the rabbit who had been good all day, keeping out of sight. He glared at the brigand. "Don't take another step," he warned. He felt the zombie pushing into his consciousness.

To his surprise, the man quailed. His knees buckled convincingly, but Lance wondered if it was a trick. Perhaps other brigands were nearby, waiting for the signal to pounce.

The zombie was ready. He showed the man his teeth and made a low growl.

On cue, the brigand called, "Whimsey! Neil!" but his voice was too shaky to carry for more than a few feet.

The zombie listened, and recognized prey. He would hunt it down when he was finished with the swooning girl. She was helpless, unable to run. The zombie stooped lower and encircled the white neck. He felt the pulse of her blood, the twitch of muscle fibers, the crackle of electrical current as it passed through the nerves. He began to squeeze. Yes.

"Stop! For God's sake, stop!"

It was a familiar voice. The zombie paused and looked up at the other prey—the one who had escaped him before. It was trying to escape again. The zombie followed.

cḣapter seventeen

Lance's first coherent thought was: There's a skunk snuffling around my face. His second thought: Don't move.

The skunk's fur was pungent with musk, yet it wasn't alarmed. Lance held his breath and tried to remain still, but to his horror the skunk climbed onto his chest and curled next to the rabbit.

The three of them kept their places for a full minute. It might have gone on for even longer, but the skunk started when it heard the sound of footsteps. It clambered off to investigate.

Lance could hardly believe that his luck had lasted so long. It was sure to run out soon. The skunk would take alarm and begin to go through its warning ritual: pounding the ground with its paws, hissing, and finally lifting its tail.

The skunk did none of these things. Instead it ran to the intruder—a small adult, or perhaps a child—and allowed itself to be swept into the child's arms.

Lance couldn't bear to watch anymore. He squeezed his eyes shut. "Don't come closer," he said. "You're holding a skunk. Put it down and run!"

Whoever it was began to laugh. It sounded like a woman, though he couldn't see anyone. The laughter seemed to get closer, though, and he was sure that she had taken a seat next to him.

He narrowed his eyes and caught sight of a young lady with a skunk sitting on her bended knees. He squinted at her face, and she disappeared altogether: the skunk seemed to be floating in the air. When he looked again, he saw a bit of forehead, the curl of her ear, a hand resting on the skunk's back. The images glowed for an instant, then went dark, like the last few flickers of a lightbulb just before the filament snaps.

Then she seemed to take a different form. Her features became steadier and more solid, but her color changed, merging into black and gray striations that looked just like the bark of the tree behind her. Watching her made Lance dizzy, and he must have swayed a little, because he felt her steadying hand on his shoulder.

"I'm sorry I laughed," the woman said. "It's just that no one's ever told me to run from Rhiannon." She held up the skunk as if she were introducing it.

Lance blinked rapidly, but he couldn't get her in focus.

"Are you well?" she asked.

Lance sat up, utterly confused. He didn't recognize the woman, didn't know where he was. What had happened to MrsKeller and Rayva?

The woman seemed to read his thoughts. "They're perfectly fine. Considering what they've been through. Adam is worried, though. I promised him I'd look for you. He thought you had gotten hurt while chasing off the brigand."

"I chased a brigand?" He couldn't remember doing that. He had a sinking feeling that the zombie had, and that this strange woman was trying to hunt the monster down.

He wondered how much she knew. "Were you there at the time?"

"I *should* have been: Smoke Rise is my district. Unfortunately I was patrolling elsewhere."

Lance felt sick. "What do you mean exactly when you say 'patrol'?"

"Are you sure you're quite well?" she asked. "You don't look it."

"It's my eyes. I can't really see you. Maybe the brigand hit me on the head."

"Is that so?" She didn't bother to hide her skepticism. "Is there no other reason why I might be difficult to see?"

Lance flushed with embarrassment. He began to stammer an apology, but she silenced him by touching his lips with her finger. Then she drew a circle in the air, and a spark traced the path of her fingers like a tiny flame racing along a fuse. When the circle was complete, it glowed yellow, then turned to smoke. When the smoke drifted away, Lance saw the woman's face clearly. She was smiling.

"You still don't understand?"

Lance shook his head.

"You don't recognize ordinary druid magic? Camouflage spells, illumination . . ."

He gaped at her. "You're a druid?"

"You don't know?" The woman clapped her hands in delight. "You must be a visitor." She inclined her head in a courteous bow. "I'm Beck, druid of Smoke Rise. Welcome to Earth."

"Thank you," he said, watching her eyes change from peach to violet. "I'm Lance."

She laughed again. "So I hear. And is this your first visit?"

Lance nodded as if he had been listening. Then his brain caught up with the words.

"Did you say *Earth*?"

"Certainly. Are there druids elsewhere?" She seemed to think Lance was making a joke, but when he didn't respond, her smile faded. "Every world needs its guardians. I only wish Earth had more."

Lance felt reality slipping away from him. Was the woman trying to give him some kind of test? If so, he had no time for it.

"I don't mean to be rude," he said, "but I have to go back to my friends."

"Of course." She looked stricken. "My duty is to reunite you with them, not pry into your private matters. But allow me to do one thing before we go—"

To Lance's astonishment, she picked up the rabbit, opened his pack, and dropped it inside. "In Southern Lands, keep the bunya hidden at all times. Otherwise you'll be arrested as a druid spy."

"But I'm not," Lance said. He had a hazy memory of the brigand gloating over his rabbit. "I don't know a thing about druid magic."

"No need to convince me. We druids *can tell*. Unfortunately, the rest of the world relies on appearances. Since you have a druid's bunya, you must be a druid, and worth a small fortune to any brigand or rogue. When you're turned in, the Warriors will torture you for information about the rebels and will tear your familiar to pieces in front of you. Then you'll be hanged." After a pause she added, "Your traveling companions will be tarred with the same brush, and will meet the same fate."

Lance recalled how many times the rabbit had been out in the open. "MrsKeller—Adam—already knows about the, er, bunya, but we've only just met Rayva. She hasn't seen it."

"Good. Rayva's a Penance girl, of course, but the less she knows about you, the better." The druid got to her feet. "Ready, Lance? Ready, Rhiannon?" The skunk looked up at her. Lance pulled on his pack.

Beck sent the skunk ahead to scout the route, while she reverted to heavy camouflage, guiding Lance with one hand on his arm. She moved with confidence, finding her way through the ancient trees without the help of moonlight or even a path.

Beck seemed to float above the ground as she walked, but Lance managed to step on every dry leaf and twig. He tried to walk the way the druid did, and was so absorbed in the motion of his feet that he smacked his head against a low branch.

Tactfully, Beck began to make conversation. "We'll soon be at Smoke Rise, which we maintain as a shelter for Penance travelers. I'll be leaving once I see you settled, but if you wouldn't mind, I'd love to hear something about your world. Is it very different from Earth?"

Lance's forehead was still throbbing from the tree, and he was too tired to invent a story. "*I'm* from Earth," he said. "At least that's what we call it. But it's nothing like Discordia—and we have no druids, except in books—and in games."

She patted his hand. "I think you've mixed things up, and no wonder after your tiring day. Discordia must be your world."

Lance shrugged. He *was* tired, and he heard the river in the distance. Suddenly all he wanted to do was find MrsKeller and Rayva, and go to sleep.

The druid didn't press him for more conversation until they were close enough to the river to hear the rapids.

"While Rayva was sleeping, MrsKeller and I had a brief chat. He didn't tell me much, but when he heard me discussing plans with Rayva, he hinted that your road takes you to the Dark Weald Peninsula."

Lance nodded.

"He seemed to think that you wouldn't mind traveling there with Rayva—just as far as the isthmus that connects the Weald to the Northern Lands. He wouldn't commit to it without speaking to you first, though."

"We're going there anyway—" Lance said.

"Listen to everything before you make up your mind. Rayva will be in mortal peril as long as she wears the collar. First she must go to the guild mistress of the rogues to have it removed—"

"But Rayva said that was impossible."

The druid sighed. "In Liander, anything is possible with the right kind of bribe—and I have given Rayva a bribe that can open many doors. When the collar is gone, you must go to the Weald as fast as you can manage, and then see her across the isthmus and to the Northern Lands. She'll make her way from there." She paused. "Are you willing to face this danger for the sake of a runaway slave?"

"I'm willing if MrsKeller is. Seems crazy to make her go alone when we have to take the trip anyway."

"I'm very glad," Beck said. "None of us can enter the

city at the moment, and I haven't been through there in months."

Beck had to raise her voice so that Lance could hear her. They were nearly at the river. It sounded excessively loud in his ears, louder than it had been near the towns. When they got to the end of the path he saw why: the river had become a waterfall.

She indicated that they were to continue on a ledge ten feet below the top of the falls. He followed, but just before she set foot on the slick stone, he touched her shoulder and bent down to speak in her ear.

"Do we have to go that way?" He tried not to look at the churning white basin three stories below them. "I get a little nervous about heights."

"There's no other way," she said. "You can hold my hand if you like."

Lance felt his gut twist into a knot, but he assured the druid that he would be fine. They ducked behind the curtain of water. The ledge was wet with spray and slimy moss, and he had to force himself to edge along with his back to the stone.

Halfway across, Beck disappeared around a bulge of rock. Lance went after her, and was immensely glad to see her waiting for him at the entrance to a cave. She gestured him inside. With a shudder of relief, Lance flung himself over the threshold and found himself standing in a rounded cavern less than twelve feet in diameter—a circular divot in a mica cliff that supported the falls. Screens of plaited reeds kept off the damp, and there was a thick layer of moss on the floor. A basin of fire kept the room warm, and near it was a stone table covered with loaves of brown bread, a round of cheese, and a basket of apples.

MrsKeller had been poking the fire, but when he saw that

Lance had come, he threw down the stick and gave him an exuberant hug. Rayva was resting in the corner, but she noticed him too, and smiled shyly.

Beck tried to tell him something, but he couldn't hear her. The druid returned to the mouth of the cave and showed him a sliding wooden door. She closed off the entrance, and the cacophony of water faded away.

"Oh, that's much better," Rayva said. Then she lay her head down and closed her eyes.

"I've given her some herbs to help her sleep," Beck told him. "She needs a good night's rest to get to the next safe place— the druid's tree." She nodded at Rayva, who was already sleeping. "She'll recognize it, of course, and I've cast a spell on its branches to shield you from harm. The spell is for tomorrow night only, so don't lose your way."

Lance was a little anxious about the vagueness of the plan. "You're sure that Rayva will know which tree it is?"

The druid raised her eyebrows. "Who on Earth can fail to recognize a druid tree?"

MrsKeller discreetly raised his hand.

"The rest of the plan you know. I've left you food, instructions, and the bribe, but I shouldn't stay any longer." She signaled to the skunk, and it jumped into to her arms. She pressed the children's hands, wished them luck, and uttered the familiar battle cry: "They shall pay Penance."

The boys responded, "And their names will be forgotten."

As the druid slipped through the door, Lance realized that for the first time, he and MrsKeller had spoken the Penance chant. In the real Discordia, they had switched sides.

Cɦɑpτeʀ Eiɢɦτeeɲ

Rayva woke up and stared at the crumbling gray ash in the fire basin. Even after the herb-induced sleep, she didn't need to see the sunrise to know when it was time to begin the day's work. She was conditioned to this routine, but the two lads were not. They were stretched out beneath their cloaks, and neither one showed the slightest inclination to stir.

Rayva's head throbbed with a soft steady ache, and there was a bad taste in her mouth from the druid's sleeping potion. She was thirsty, but she walked right past the lads' fine water skins. She slid open the heavy door, stepped onto the ledge, and scooped up handfuls of icy water from the pounding falls. It was cold enough to make her throat spasm and her teeth ache, but it tasted so pure that she could hardly stop drinking it.

Finally she'd had enough, and she thrust her arms into the falls, feeling the water stream down on either side of her hands. When that became too painful, she dipped her face into the cascade and gently scooped some water over the lump at the base of her skull. An icy rivulet ran down her back, and she stepped away, shivering with cold. Her dripping hair soaked the back of her tunic, but her cheeks glowed red as the blood raced through her—the last residue of the druid's potion washed away.

If only she could banish the dreams that had pursued her all night: a nauseating swirl of blue, an endless race through a dark cavern, and the sad, thin face of the tall lad—Lance—gazing at her with hungry eyes that were the same deep brown color of Aster's topaz ring. She saw his face moving closer, looming over hers, and the brown eyes bulging and writhing with maggots. His skin was turning gray and hanging loose from the bones, and his mouth stank of the grave.

At one point she'd called out and woken herself up, but the boys were heavy sleepers and hadn't heard her. She'd looked over at Lance's angular limbs sticking out from his cloak, and had tried to laugh off the dream. He was excessively thin—practically all bones—but that didn't make him a ravenous corpse. He was just a boy who had shot up fast, and who'd feel much better about life after he had a few good meals.

She walked into the cave, shut the door behind her, and carried some fresh kindling for the fire from the pile near the doorway. She coaxed a flame from a lone hot ember and fed it carefully. Soon it roared back to life, and her wet clothing steamed in the heat.

She looked up and caught Adam looking at her quizzically. She met his glance with a look of her own. Why did Lance call him Missus Keller all the time? That sounded like a girl's name, and there was nothing girlie about him. She thought he was very handsome, though the Seyrens would be suspicious of anyone with such an unusual appearance. None of the villagers had dark skin and green eyes, and they'd probably assume that MrsKeller was from a Northern clan.

That wouldn't make her nervous, of course. Northern people were the most trustworthy of all, and she felt sure that MrsKeller was Northern through and through. He hadn't appeared in a single one of her nightmares.

When the boys woke up, they all began to tidy the cave for the next travelers. She felt shy with these strangers, and it was good to have something to do to cover up the awkward silences.

MrsKeller started out by asking how she was feeling. She told him that she felt much better. The boys were glad to hear it, and when she asked them how they felt, they both said that they were well. Then the conversation lagged until they ate breakfast and left the cave.

Rayva smiled as they passed beneath the rushing water, but she noticed that Lance hung back. When he got to the end of the ledge, he sprang out into the fresh air with great enthusiasm, just as she had done. Rayva guessed that Lance must be savoring every moment just as she was, and thrilling to every step into the unknown.

She tried to stay calm, though she was continually overwhelmed by ordinary things that the lads took for granted. When she saw the view from Smoke Rise, it took her breath away. For the first time the world was spread out before her. It seemed huge and tiny at the same time. The river cut through countless miles of forests and fields—a darting blue snake that bisected lonely green valleys and squares of farmland. At its head was Liander, the largest city on Earth, but if Rayva closed one eye she could cover it with her thumb.

She knew they were many miles from the city, yet she could discern the smoke from hundreds of cooking fires. She pointed these out to the boys. "Now I understand why they call this view Smoke Rise."

"I do believe you're right," MrsKeller said with an easy smile. "That hadn't occurred to me."

She must have looked shocked when he said this, because he turned to her with great concern and asked if she was feeling sick again. How kindhearted he was!

Lance only stared at her collar: he seemed to understand what she was thinking.

Rayva tried to explain what it meant to hear a freeman speak to her as if she were his equal, but MrsKeller seemed almost angry that she could consider herself anything less.

"Equal?" he spluttered. "Better than equal. I heard you tell the druid about shooting that plague beast with a regular old bow and arrow—after all you had been through, and that crazy swim . . ." He looked at her with genuine admiration. "I've done some bow hunting with my *grand-père*. I used to think I was pretty good, but you make me look like the biggest noob on earth."

She had to laugh at his odd way of talking. It was hard to understand, but she knew he meant well.

The three of them followed the path downhill, scrambling over rocks as they headed for the valley far below. Mile after mile they walked along the river. They passed no other travelers, and though the trip was uneventful, they weren't completely at ease. Peace was making them anxious, and one of them always seemed to hear the sound of hoofbeats in the distance, or the jingle of chain mail.

In the late afternoon their progress slowed. The path was choked with knotweed, which was smothering the birch trees that leaned over the water. Only one tree had resisted the deadly growth: an ordinary-looking willow that was still in full leaf.

"That's it," Rayva said. "It has to be."

They slipped between the swaying frondlike branches and looked around with wondering eyes. The willow's delicate leaves made an odd contrast with the graceless trunk, which was thick enough to support an oak tree three times its size. Thin rays of sunlight filtered in, turning the small enclosure emerald. It smelled sweet—of honeysuckle and freshly cut hay.

Rayva sat down and touched the back of her head gingerly. "I forgot that I wasn't supposed to braid my hair this morning." She began to undo it. "Only slaves bind their hair."

"Looks nice either way," MrsKeller said.

She smiled. "The only thing I care about is looking like a freewoman."

They went down to the water to replenish their empty skins. Night was closing in, and they were surrounded by an increasing number of gleaming eyes.

"Let's finish this job in the morning," Lance said. "Those animals might be hungry."

Rayva laughed. "The little nighttime rangers?" She clapped her hands and lunged toward them. The eyes drew back. "Why are you worried about *them*?"

"Never saw them before," Lance said as they ducked back under the willow branches.

"What?" Rayva drew herself up short. "You've never seen them outside your village?"

She noticed the boys exchanging uncomfortable looks. They had done this a few times that day, especially when she asked about their villages and families.

She added, "I don't mean to pry if you'd rather not say."

"You're not prying," Lance said. "Not at all. But the druid told us that we shouldn't talk about where we're from, or what we're doing. She thinks you'll be safer that way."

Rayva shrugged. "If that's what Beck said—" She was disappointed, but she had to accept the druid's opinion. Beck would know best, and if all went well, she wouldn't have to wait much longer until learning about the North firsthand.

The three of them settled down for the night, but Rayva was too restless to sleep, and she didn't like the rustling sounds she heard near the tree. She parted the branches. The air felt sharp and cold on her skin, and she thought she heard the muffled thud of hoofbeats. Was it a horse out there—or a plague beast?

Rayva stepped back quickly and watched the branches close. Beck had said that her spell would keep them safe for the night—why should she doubt her word? Rayva lay down again and pulled the cloak over her head. Gradually she relaxed, cocooned in a little bubble of warm air. She sighed with contentment and fell asleep, dreaming that she was already home.

They awoke to a perfect, shining blue day. Rayva stepped through the branches and stood on the riverbank, admiring the dappled light on the water.

"I guess we survived the night." MrsKeller stretched his

arms over his head and yawned. "Lady Willow must have decided that we needed our beauty sleep."

"That was beauty sleep?" Lance said. "If it was, you need another eight hours."

"Speak for yourself," said MrsKeller. "You could use another twenty-four." He raised his voice and called, "Don't you agree, Rayva?"

She laughed and stepped through the branches. "I have no idea what you're talking about, and I don't care."

MrsKeller tried to get her to eat some bread and cheese, but she refused. "I'm too excited," she said. "All I want to do is get to the city, pay the entrance tax, and walk in like a freewoman."

Abruptly, she stopped and turned to Lance. "Would you mind letting me have a few coins for my purse? I have nothing but the brooch Beck gave me."

Lance pulled the whole purse off his belt and tried to make her wear it, but she would only accept twenty coppers. "That's plenty," she said. "More than I've had in my whole life."

They set out along the river path in a lighthearted mood. Rayva had one bad moment when she caught herself laughing and turning from one boy to the other, and she suddenly felt as if she had changed places with Aster. She pictured the plague beast charging toward them, and squeezed her eyes shut, but then she heard Adam and Lance exchanging one of their odd jokes, and she felt herself again.

Wisps of clouds drifted across a clear sky. The land rose and fell in gentle hills that were covered with small, scrubby pines. The tops of the hills were bare, but Lance could see small light-covered objects moving on them. "Sheep?"

Rayva suggested that they might just as easily be goats.

"Either way," said Lance, "it must mean that we're still far from the city."

"Why?" Rayva said with some surprise. "I'm sure they have both in Liander. Every town has both."

Lance looked down and saw that the road beneath their feet had widened and was paved with large flat stones. "I'm not sure about that. Liander might be more built up than you think."

A steady stream of people toiled upward, most of them on foot and pushing handcarts, though some were riding horses or mules. All stopped briefly at a wooden hut where a toll keeper collected a tax for entering the city.

When the three approached the hut, Lance gazed down and saw the toll keeper: a man who stood about four feet high. His shoulders were broad and his belly was broader, and his arms were so muscled that he couldn't stand with them at his sides but had to hold them away from his body. His eyebrows were almost bushy enough to obscure his small eyes, and he had a thick brown beard that was twisted into three matted braids.

"Good morning, travelers."

"Good morning," they chorused.

"Here to visit the lovely city of Liander?"

"We are indeed, sir," Rayva said. She reached into her purse and dug out three copper pieces.

"What's this?" the dwarf said, eyeing them suspiciously. "I see but three in your hand. Where is the copper for yon lads?"

Rayva remembered what Beck had told her. "Three

coppers is what the fare has always been—one copper for each traveler," she said firmly.

"Times have changed, and revenue must be raised," the dwarf replied. "His Majesty, the good King Lair the Builder, now demands three coppers per person."

"That's robbery," MrsKeller said. "Why, you just raised the price when you saw the coppers in her hand."

"And who would *you* be? The king's new bailiff?" The toll keeper's lips twisted into an ugly sneer.

"Nothing like that," MrsKeller said hastily. "Just a traveler. I thought it was one copper per person. Or per dwarf, or whatever."

"The toll is what I say it is," the dwarf said, drawing himself up as tall as he could manage. "Am I not the royal toll collector and guardian of this road?"

"Maybe so," MrsKeller said, "but that doesn't mean you have the right to raise the price any time you feel like it."

"Does it not? You forget that I need not let you in if I don't like your looks. And I'm beginning to think that I don't care for them at all."

MrsKeller waved his hands as if trying to erase his side of the conversation. "We'll pay. I was only saying . . ."

Lance elbowed MrsKeller sharply in the ribs.

". . . I was only saying that we'd be glad to pay the tariff," he amended.

"Sure you wouldn't rather enter for nothing, under the arm of a royal guard? The dungeons are nice and damp this season. Freshly watered, or so I've heard."

Rayva dug out another six coppers. "We don't want any trouble."

The dwarf snatched the extra coins and held them to the light. For good measure he put one between his front teeth and clamped down hard.

"Go on, then," he said, waving his hand irritably. "Why do you lollygag around here?"

They didn't wait to be asked a second time. As soon as the dwarf turned his back on them, they resumed their rapid stride.

The road took a sharp turn and gave them their first clear view of Liander. Dark gray walls and towers perched on top of a cliff, like a crown, and seemed to stare down at the travelers as if promising to crush anyone who dared assault its borders.

To enter the city they had to cross a dry moat by way of a drawbridge. Rows of soldiers in plumed helmets and chain mail stood guard, holding eight-foot-long spears. Their faces were blank, perhaps stiff with boredom, but Lance had no doubt that they'd spring to action quickly enough, if need be.

Lance kept his head down as they passed through the open gates and didn't look up until he stood in the vast courtyard just within the city walls. Dozens of narrow streets radiated from this point, and they gazed around in bewilderment, wondering where to go. A tiny, stumping figure lurched toward them—using his arms to propel himself. The man's legs were shrunken and deformed, hardly more than clubbed feet projecting from his torso.

"Alms for a crust of bread, kind maiden. Alms, good able-bodied youths. Help a poor cripple who has had nowt but a mouthful of gruel the whole livelong day."

"Here you are, father." Rayva reached into her purse and gave him a few coppers.

The beggar examined the copper pieces. "Thank you, my daughter. Blessings upon you for taking pity on a poor cripple."

"You're very welcome," she answered.

The beggar stared. "I've never seen anyone part with money so gladly," he said. "You can't possibly be from Liander."

"We're not," Rayva said. "We're only here to see the mistress of the rogues' guild, but we don't know where to find her."

"A country girl like you?" he said disapprovingly. "What kind of business would you have with her?"

MrsKeller cut Rayva's answer short. "Our *own*, if you don't mind."

The beggar shrugged. "Then I suppose you know *where* your business is."

He turned away in a huff, but Lance stopped him with a flash of silver. "We really could use a guide."

The beggar stretched out his hand and cackled. "And I really could use a silver." He quickly slipped the coin into a purse hidden beneath his shirt. "Follow me, please, and don't wander off. The city's no place for children like you."

He led them to an open square dominated by three empty pavilions. Lance wondered aloud what they might be used for.

The beggar gaped. "You don't know?"

Lance admitted that he didn't.

"Nor even heard about how we do things on market days?"

Lance shook his head, hoping the beggar wouldn't probe further.

Luckily the beggar supplied the details himself. "You must be from one of the mountain towns," he said, sneering. "It sticks out a league."

MrsKeller stifled a laugh. "So true. Everyone knows that the villagers come from miles around to buy and sell. Nothing tops the Liander fairs."

"Right you are, lad. And the biggest fair is our autumn festival, exactly a fortnight from today. There'll be hundreds of merchants converging on the city, hoping to make a profit. The tanners will show their best leather and their finest skins, the shepherds will display their best wool to tempt the weavers, the artisans will bring their best tools—you'd get dizzy seeing all the buying and selling." He rubbed his hands together. "And the wine and beer merchants sell their wares night and day, and people will be eager to give a poor cripple a few coppers."

"Too bad we'll have to miss it this time," said MrsKeller, winking at Lance over the beggar's head. "It may be a while before we can get back."

The beggar shrugged. "Well, since you're here, you can get a taste of the fine things just by walking the trade district."

He led them through a street where every building contained a workshop or storeroom. Customers stood outside and bought what they needed at the counter beneath a window that was shielded by an awning overhead. It looked like anything that could be bought and sold was on display: fabrics, jewelry, boots, weapons, dishware, silver, hats, robes, medicines, rugs, furs, toys, wigs, good-luck charms—all in an amazing profusion of colors and styles. And at the end of the day, the counters and awnings folded against the window like shutters, protecting the shop within.

Rayva's step slowed, and she turned to examine the delicate kid gloves displayed on one counter and the softly shining silver brooches and bracelets on another. The beggar caught Rayva's eye and gave an abrupt, barking laugh. "Pretty baubles for a pretty maid."

Rayva blushed. "I've never seen so many fine things."

"Aye, and there are folks here who have gold enough to buy them." He pointed to a three-story building with a red tile roof. "You see that?"

Rayva craned her neck and looked up. "How many people live there?"

The beggar pursed his lips thoughtfully. "Could be that it belongs to just one family and their servants."

"Can it be true?" Rayva exclaimed. "Three entire levels for their own use?"

The beggar shrugged. "If they are rich. But most of us are glad for shelter and two meals a day."

They turned down another street that was just as bustling, though not quite as prosperous. The shops here were devoted to food: onions, leeks, winter squash, bread and pastries, eggs, cheese, milk and butter, oil, honey, and spices. There was even a shop that offered live poultry and rabbits for the cooking pot. The animals had their legs trussed, and flopped around in a futile attempt to break free. A woman in a rough-spun tunic and long cloak hefted a goose and gave it a good pinch to determine how plump it was. The outraged bird nearly split the air with its hoarse cries, and all the passersby laughed.

"Now, in these buildings there live a number of families," the beggar explained, "mayhap one family per floor, because the folks are not as rich. Still, they'll do, compared to how most of us live."

They walked beneath a brightly painted wooden sign depicting a wild boar playing the pan pipes. "The Pig and Whistle," the beggar said. "They serve a decent mug of ale here, and travelers can get a good straw mattress, if they don't mind the company."

"What company is that?" MrsKeller asked.

"Fleas mostly. And lice. And bedbugs." The beggar roared at his own witticism and paused to wipe his eyes.

Rayva whispered to MrsKeller, "That's the inn that Beck told us about—the one closest to the road that leads to the Seagate."

Lance tried to memorize landmarks that would help them get back to this spot. As long as they remained in the market district, Lance was fairly confident they'd find the inn easily; but after five minutes in the adjoining slums, he lost his bearings altogether. The roads degenerated into twisted paths that snaked around crudely built wattle-and-daub shanties. A few grubby children worked narrow strips of garden, competing with roaming chickens and pigs for anything that might be edible. Idle youths were trying to drum up excitement by staging dogfights, or setting fire to cats, or simply harassing passersby.

Lance noticed four bare-legged boys in ragged tunics trailing after a wretched-looking knife grinder who was hawking his services in a loud singsong chant: "Knife grinding, knife grinding. Get your blades sharpened for just two coppers. Knife grinding, knife grinding."

The knife grinder looked as shabby and downtrodden as the boys who shouted over his chant, but at least the boys were enjoying themselves. The knife grinder's face was blank, stupefied, and hopeless. Except for the obnoxious little gang that slouched behind him, no one paid him a bit of attention. Perhaps the people here had no knives at all.

At last the beggar halted in front of a house at the very end of the street, leaning on the city wall. He knocked on a dented pine door, which was flung open by a woman so tall she had to duck to clear the lintel. She thrust her head outside and eyed them suspiciously.

"What now, Higdor?" she said to the beggar.

"Visitors to see Guild Mistress Maevis."

"And their business?" she asked, staring pointedly at MrsKeller's Ship's Ahoy shirt.

"Nothing they cared to share with me."

The woman started to close the door. "Then good day to you."

Rayva thrust out her foot to keep the door open, reaching into her purse at the same time.

"Allow us to show our gratitude for your kindness," she said, slipping something into the woman's hands. The door, as if on its own, opened wide.

"And to you as well, Higdor." Rayva placed another coin in his outstretched hand.

He stared at the copper and tugged on a forelock to show his thanks. "I'll leave you, then," he said with a sly smile. "And may you find what you seek at journey's end."

Chapter Nineteen

*T*he woman grudgingly shoved them into a small room. A large cauldron of soup bubbled over an open pit. The burning embers cast a fitful red glow that illuminated the woman's face as she bent down to stir the pot. She seemed to have forgotten about them.

Rayva spoke up. "Excuse me, mother, we're here to see the guild mistress."

The woman growled, "State your business or I'll toss you out into the street."

Rayva wondered if the woman was angling for a second bribe. She and the boys exchanged glances, and Lance was about to reach into his purse when a sharp voice said, "Nime, show the visitors into my chambers."

The servant was so startled she dropped her spoon into the depths of the cauldron. She wheeled around and curtsied deeply without bothering to wipe away the splashes of soup that dripped on her dress.

"But, Guild Mistress," she said, "you told me . . ." Her words trailed off.

"Just send them through."

The servant stepped aside, and Rayva caught a glimpse of the rapidly retreating figure of the guild mistress. Before she had a chance to wonder if Nime was to accompany them, the woman barked out an order without bothering to turn around.

"This way," she said. "Follow me."

They entered a second room lit only by two windows draped with yellowed parchment. In the center was a large table covered with heavy metal boxes, and an elaborately carved chair with a high back. The guild mistress obviously preferred to keep her visitors standing: there was no other place to sit.

She indicated that they should line up along the table, then she scrutinized each one of them. "Which of you wanted to see me?"

Rayva tried to curtsy the way the servant had, but she did it awkwardly, unnerved by the guild mistress's harsh, authoritarian manner. The woman's chiseled features seemed to have been carved from the same dark wood as the chair, and were just as unyeilding.

Rayva quailed at the thought of asking for help. The woman's eyes were empty. There was no sympathy—not even a drop of human kindness. If the guild mistress scorned the diamond brooch, Rayva felt sure they'd be thrown into the street—if they were lucky. If the guild mistress thought that she'd profit by their arrest, she'd certainly hand them over to the Warriors without a second thought.

Rayva opened her purse with trembling fingers. She removed the brooch but kept it hidden in her palm.

After attempting another curtsy, she said, "I apologize for

coming unannounced, but I need something done that requires great skill, and I think you are the only who has it." In a quick gesture she pulled off the scarf that hid her collar. "Can you unlock such a thing?"

The guild mistress looked at her severely. "That would be tampering with the law—a capital offense."

Rayva let her fingers uncurl and tilted her hand to let the facets of the diamonds catch the light. Maevis's eyes widened.

"On the other hand," she said, "so many people are wrongly accused, and I hate to see such a young girl live her life in slavery." She beckoned Rayva to come closer, then plucked the brooch from her hand. After examining it carefully, she reached into a hidden pocket in the sleeve of her dress and withdrew a square of white velvet that contained a dozen lock picks.

She held up her hand for silence, and for nearly half an hour she worked on Rayva's collar with slow, patient movements. After an eternity of quiet scratching and scrapings, Maevis gave the collar a final twist, and it fell open, clattering to the floor.

Rayva felt her bare neck with disbelief and gasped. "Thank you, Guild Mistress."

Maevis dismissed her with a contemptuous glance and turned her attention to the boys, who had been watching from the side. "And do you have business here as well, lads?"

"Not anymore," MrsKeller said quickly. He took Rayva by the arm and began to steer her out of the room. "We'll just be on our way."

Nime was waiting for them in the hallway. She led them back to the center room, jostled them outside, and slammed the door after them.

"Whew," MrsKeller said softly. "I don't think she cares for us at all. What do you think?"

He had directed the question to Rayva, but she didn't hear him. Tears spilled down her cheeks. She tried to wipe them away, first on one sleeve and then the other, but they kept coming. She sniffled loudly but managed to give Lance a wan smile when he offered the use of his cloak as a handkerchief.

"It's gone," she said tremulously. "And we got out of there alive."

"For now, anyway." MrsKeller looked around furtively. "She seems like the kind of gal who might change her mind pretty easy, don't you think?"

Lance nodded emphatically. "Best thing we can do is find the Pig and Whistle and lie low until tomorrow morning. I'm not going to relax until I see the coast of the Dark Weald."

The streets around the guild house were more crowded now. It was getting close to dusk, and the people who lived in the slums were straggling home after a long day. Most of the faces were rigid with exhaustion, but two thickset, muscular men provided some free entertainment by having a noisy argument over a large eel. To the delight of the crowd, one of the men won his point by snatching the eel away and using it to whip his opponent across the face.

A group of children tried to worm their way to the front to see what was happening, but they couldn't get through. Deprived of the entertainment, they began fights of their own. Two little boys began to wrestle. One was thrown off balance and fell against Lance, nearly knocking him over.

MrsKeller grabbed Lance with one arm, wrapped the other around Rayva's shoulders, and propelled them away from the crowd. They tried to retrace their steps back to the trade district, but must have made a wrong turn. They walked down a narrow street lined with dreary little shacks that leaned against each other as if exhausted. A small dog chased after them, yelping with excitement.

A butcher's apprentice appeared wearing a bloody leather apron. He was no more than ten or eleven, and was barely able to stagger beneath the weight of a large basin. The contents sloshed noisily. Instantly a semicircle of bony mutts gathered, tensely jockeying for position with fangs bared.

The boy yelped in fear and dumped the steaming entrails onto the cobblestones. The little dog that had chased them launched itself into the center of the pile and gave them all a happy glance, its muzzle dripping crimson.

It wasn't an unusual scene, but Rayva couldn't help noticing the strange effect it was having on Lance. He was intensely interested in the dog, though to Rayva it looked like a perfectly ordinary mongrel with rough yellow fur that stuck out in all directions.

The longer Lance stared at the dog, the worse he appeared. His face had become a mottled green color. The mongrel seemed aware of Lance's scrutiny, and it showed off its cleverness by rolling in the gore.

Lance turned away as if he were going to be sick. Perhaps he was squeamish; yet for one split second, Rayva had the confused impression that Lance's skin was flapping loose over his skull, as if his face were a sheet hung up to dry. She looked again, but he was gone, careening through the street and splashing through piles of refuse and dark puddles of murky liquid. Rayva and MrsKeller ran after him.

Lance darted into a narrow space between two buildings. MrsKeller got nearly close enough to grab his cloak, but Rayva had fallen behind. By the time she reached the alley, she could no longer see either of them. She walked through it as quickly as she could. It stank like a urinal and was littered with construction debris: chunks of fallen plaster, broken saplings, and moldy thatch. The shadows and stale air made her feel faint. Her head throbbed, and she hoped that she would get to the other side before passing out.

She stumbled along, touching each wall to steady herself. She squinted at the rectangle of fading daylight at the end of the alley: it seemed a long way off. She made an effort to quicken her pace, but something forced her to draw up short. Had her cloak snagged on something?

She looked up and saw two young brigands, a man and a woman, in leather and chain mail. The woman had very short white-blond hair, and a silver-handled throwing knife that she tossed from hand to hand. Rayva's heart beat like a frenzied animal trying to break free of her chest, but she tried to seem calm and unconcerned.

"Seen a couple of lads run past?" Unconsciously, Rayva's hand inched toward the scabbard of her hunting knife, poised to defend herself.

In an instant the man closed his fingers over her wrist. He pulled her toward him and gave her a good look at his crooked yellow teeth. He started to laugh. "Hey, don't bother, sister. The scabbard's empty."

Rayva flushed, half angered, half mortified that she had been caught doing something so pointless—her knife had been stolen by a brigand days ago. The real weapon was the stiletto in her boot. She'd never be able to reach it now.

The male brigand gave her an appraising look. "Lookee who we've got here, Whimsey. Isn't this the girl with the strange friends?"

"The very same," the woman said. "Every single brigand in the city has been talking about that odd little threesome, and here's one of them right in our path, looking for the tall one and his friend."

Rayva pretended not to have understood their teasing, and asked again if they had seen anyone run through the alley.

"You mean the dark lad with the long hair?" the woman said.

"That's right," Rayva said. "And . . ." She trailed off. Instead of picturing her friend, she saw the monstrous creature from her dreams. Is that what she was trying to find?

"And? And?" The woman eyed Rayva impatiently. "And did we also notice the tall lad too?"

Rayva nodded, and the woman elbowed the man in the ribs. "Yeah, we saw him—but are you sure you actually want to find him?" She opened her eyes as wide as she could to show how astonished she was.

Rayva stared back without emotion. "Of course I want to find them. Otherwise I wouldn't have asked."

The woman bent forward. "If I were you, I wouldn't hang around with them," she whispered. "Our friend Duncan swears that the tall lad can turn himself into a monster."

"Not a monster, Whimsey. A walking corpse. Who actually tried to throttle *you*," he said, gesturing at Rayva.

"Duncan says they're Penance spies," the man continued, watching Rayva closely for a reaction.

Rayva tried to keep the panic off her face. If the brigands really thought the lads were spies, they might have been arrested already—and she'd be next.

"I know nothing of Penance," Rayva said coldly. "I have to go now."

The woman and man made *tsk-tsk*ing sounds and shook their heads in disbelief, but they let her push past them.

Rayva walked away with quick, purposeful steps. Her mind was racing, and she was uncomfortably aware that the brigands were trailing after her. She heard the man say in a pitying tone, "And she doesn't even have a weapon."

The woman laughed. "Probably doesn't matter. How can you kill a walking corpse?"

Finally, Rayva got to the end of the alley. As soon as her feet hit the cobblestones, she started to run.

MrsKeller wheeled around to face Lance. "Why'd you take off like that?" he demanded.

"You think I had a choice?" Lance leaned against the corner of a building, suddenly exhausted. "The zombie was trying to take over. Didn't you see?"

MrsKeller slung an arm around Lance's shoulders. "Maybe just a touch. Not so much that Rayva noticed."

"Just a touch?" What in the world did that mean? A slightly

decayed nose? A small bloom of maggots in his cheek? A certain absence of lip? Lance groaned.

"Nobody's perfect, bud," MrsKeller said. "And I'll bet you that Rayva's on her way to the Pig and Whistle, just like we planned. If we don't hurry, she'll get there first."

Lance didn't believe it, but he quickened his step, just in case. The streets were quieter now. Shopkeepers were folding up their counters and locking their shutters for the day, and the buildings began to look like rows of blank faces with closed eyes. From the second stories the windows glowed with lamps and cooking fires, and the air was overlaid with the sulfurous smell of boiling cabbage and onions.

A group of children swarmed around the boys, their bare feet pounding the cobbles, their hands out. Two of the youngest raised their arms beseechingly. "Misters, misters—coppers, coppers. We're hungry!"

The sharp, dirty faces surrounding Lance were more predatory than stricken. He put a few coins into their filthy hands. The children screamed and asked for more, until a door opened. A veiled woman rang a dinner bell, and the children ran to her, laughing and holding their coppers aloft.

Lance and MrsKeller exchanged mortified glances and quickly turned the corner. Soon they heard the mingled sounds of laughing, singing, and metal tankards drumming on wooden tables. On the opposite side of the narrow street was the only shop still open for business. The doors and windows had been thrown wide to exhale blasts of air redolent of unwashed bodies, fermented mash, smoke, and roasting meat.

Could Rayva be one of the patrons crammed into the long,

low room? They'd have to plunge into the crowd and make inquiries. Lance had most of the money, so Rayva would have to be waiting in the common room. With trepidation they edged in and looked at every face.

Two kegs were positioned to the left of an enormous fireplace that burned logs eight feet long. A fat sheep roasted over a pile of glowing coals. It was being tended by a six-year-old whose face was crimson from his proximity to the fire. Suspended on the other side of the fireplace was a cauldron filled with bubbling soup.

MrsKeller sniffed the air appreciatively. "Man, maybe I'm hallucinating, but that actually smells good. Kind of exotic."

Lance caught a whiff and started to laugh. "Exotic? Adam, that's New England clam chowder. I swear it is."

Lance realized that he had an aching hollow in his gut, which was decidedly hunger. They squeezed onto a bench next to a sturdy young woman, who got up as soon as they sat down. She left the remains of her meal on the table.

A hollow-cheeked woman, half hidden by a pillar, hurled herself at the plate and parked her legs beneath the table. She began to spread yellow butter on flour-dusted rolls. Her movements were rapid, almost desperate, and she focused on the bread as if nothing else existed in the world. When the last bit of butter was scraped from the dish, she crammed one of the rolls into her mouth, which was so full she could barely chew, closing her eyes in ecstasy.

Lance couldn't tear his eyes away. He wanted to slide her a few coins so she could order a proper meal, but he wondered if she'd be offended.

MrsKeller gave him a nudge and pointed toward a table full of men and women who looked to be in their early twenties, with flushed faces and disheveled hair. They were the rowdiest bunch in the room, shouting over each other to be heard, banging tankards and calling for ale and cider.

"Isn't that Rayva?" MrsKeller asked.

"With *those* people?"

"Not them," MrsKeller said. "Past the table—in the doorway."

Lance lifted himself halfway out of his seat and stared at a small, hooded figure. "Can't tell. Why don't you find out, and I'll try to get us a room, okay?"

MrsKeller nodded. "Where should we meet?"

"Outside. I'll come to you, then we'll go to the room together."

MrsKeller pushed away from the table, and Lance followed, pausing just long enough to give the hungry woman a few silver coins. He made his way to the corner of the room, where the innkeeper stood dispensing drinks and keeping an eye on the food.

A man with a dark hood over his head sidled up to the bubbling cauldron of soup. He reached into his sleeve, withdrew a long-handled spoon, and dipped it surreptitiously into the pot.

The innkeeper strode to the cauldron and wiped his hands on the white apron that stretched over his big belly. He knocked the spoon out of the hooded man's hand.

"Off with you, Gareth, before I turn you over to the Warriors."

"Wasn't doing nothing," the hooded man said. "Is it a crime to give the pot a stir?"

"Stirring is one thing, eating another—as you well know."

"Sure I've heard you say it often enough," the man said sullenly.

"Often enough, true. Just about every night, Gareth, yet you never seem to learn."

He gave the hooded man a push and went back to the kegs. He drew a pint of ale but kept his eyes on Gareth.

Eventually he noticed Lance. "What's it to be, lad? Food or grog?"

"A room, actually," Lance said.

The innkeeper tapped the keg quickly. "Sorry. Full up."

Lance's voice rose in alarm. "Nothing at all? I can pay." He opened his purse and pulled out a handful of coins.

The innkeeper was suddenly more attentive. "Six silvers and you can sleep in the stable."

"I'll take it," Lance said.

The innkeeper pocketed the money. "Go out the door and turn right." After a moment's reflection he tossed Lance a fat loaf of dark bread. "There you go, lad. Pleasant dreams."

Chapter Twenty

L ance felt a surge of relief when he saw Rayva outside, but one look at her face and he knew something bad had happened. Her expression was wooden, and she refused to meet his eyes. When he explained the arrangements, she listened impassively and fell into step with MrsKeller.

Lance pushed open the stable door and stepped inside, assailed by the warm, sleepy smell of hay and manure. The only occupants were two sturdy cart horses and a stable boy who was curled up and snoring in the corner. The boy stirred when they opened the door but didn't wake up.

MrsKeller selected a clean, empty stall on the far left. Rayva went straight in and sat down next to him, hunched over her knees. She still wouldn't look at Lance, who lingered at the half gate, wondering what was wrong.

MrsKeller waved both arms over his head. "Come *in*, dude. You're on the wrong side of the stall."

Lance stepped through and sat down in the middle of the floor. Rayva shrank back to put more distance between them.

"For God's sake, Rayva—" Lance tried to throw a piece of

straw into the water trough. He missed. "What *happened* to you?" He aimed six more pieces of straw at the trough and didn't look up until one went in.

She hesitated. "I'm on my own—no friends, no family. You and MrsKeller act like you're my friends, but we've only known each other for two days. We're practically strangers."

"In minor ways, that's true." Lance was finding it difficult to meet her gaze. "But when it come down to the things that matter—"

She cut him off. "Two brigands stopped me in an alley."

"Are you okay?" he said, reaching for her arm.

She pulled away. "Fine. They already knew I had nothing worth stealing—"

MrsKeller interrupted. "Then what did they want?"

"One of their group saw us in the forest—probably the one who robbed both of us." Her voice trembled. "The brigand claims to have seen Lance turn into a flesh-eating corpse—and says that he tried to attack me."

"You don't believe that, do you?" Lance and MrsKeller locked eyes for an instant. "Brigands are criminals—that's what Beck said. They'll do or say anything that might earn them some gold."

"Stop, Lance!" Rayva covered her ears. "Don't make it worse. I saw what happened with the dog. You were starting to *change*. Do you deny it?"

Instead of answering, Lance tore open the top of his pack and reached in with both hands. Rayva flinched—expecting something horrible—but kept her eyes open. She tried to be ready, but she had never imagined this.

A bunya's twitching nose was inches away from hers. She saw her face reflected in the dark liquid eyes. If she dared, she could have stretched out her fingers and stroked the soft brown ears.

"You're a *druid*. Why didn't you say?"

Lance flushed crimson. "Because I'm not."

Rayva began to protest, but he talked right over her. "Yes, it's a bunya, and by every natural law, that makes me a druid."

"Exactly," she said.

"Problem is, it's not like that where we're from. MrsK and I are from another place—another world, to be precise—and the laws are different there."

A skeptical expression was stealing over Rayva's face.

"Listen, Rayv—" Lance stopped to take a deep breath. "I know you think that I'm lying, but just try to keep an open mind. Try to tell yourself that no matter how improbable it sounds, it could be the truth."

She looked away, but MrsKeller gave Lance an encouraging thumbs-up.

"The truth," he continued, "is just what the brigand said."

"You're a flesh-eating corpse?" Rayva's eyebrows shot up. "I don't believe it."

"I know the feeling." Lance barked one short, mirthless laugh. "I can hardly believe it myself, but sometimes I'm a zombie. That's what we call it."

She seemed to hear only part of this. "So you *did* attack me?"

Lance hesitated. "*I* didn't—but you were nearly attacked by the monster inside me."

"The monster *inside* you?" Rayva grew quiet. After a few moments she spoke again. "And you're telling me that you can't control it?"

"I'm trying, Rayva." He lifted his head and looked her straight in the eyes. "Sometimes the zombie wants to take over. I don't know how to stop him yet."

She held his glance. "I believe that, and at the same time I don't believe any of it." She shrugged her shoulders apologetically. "It's too strange, and I have so many questions."

"I can't promise to have answers; we don't know that much ourselves." Lance tried to find the right words. "I have one question for you—"

She waited for him to continue.

"The question is, knowing—or rather—not knowing all this, will you trust us as far as the Weald?"

Suddenly she smiled, making Lance's stomach turn a triple flip.

Rayva stretched a hand toward him and MrsKeller. "As far as the Weald?" She squeezed tight. "Yes—and even beyond."

Chapter Twenty-One

It seemed as though they had just fallen asleep when the stable door flew open. Someone yelled, "Whimsh! You there?"

Lance tried to catch Rayva's eye as he eased himself into a shadowy corner. His coin purse jingled.

"Whimzer?" The man in the doorway hesitated. "Zat you?"

Lance cursed silently as the man blundered toward them. The dull thud of his boots stopped abruptly at the sound of bare feet on the floor.

A second voice piped up. "Nobody here but me, Mister Duncan. Me and the horses."

Lance jabbed MrsKeller in the ribs. They both leaned forward to listen.

"I like *that*." Duncan exhaled a gust of sour wine. "Tell a woomn somethin import', and she run off in the middle. Where'd she go?"

"I haven't seen her," the boy quavered. "No one's been here all night."

"No? Then why're you here—eh?"

"I'm the stable lad, sir. Drey—from the Pig and Whistle. I have to be here."

Duncan was incredulous. "Stable? Why is Whimsey in the stable?"

"She isn't," the boy said. "Nobody—"

Duncan cut him off. "Wait, wait—it's all coming clear. Said she was going to the stables to look for spi"—he paused for a split second—"ders. That's right." The brigand began to mutter. "Don't like 'em. Whimzer do."

Lance went cold with fear. Was this Whimzer person looking for them? Was she hiding in the stable even now?

Duncan yawned noisily. "Women," he said. "Don't try to convince them of something once their mind is made up. Waste of time." He yawned again. "Landlord won't mind if I take a little kip, right, Drey?"

Lance heard the sound of a gate being opened and straw being scraped into a pile.

Duncan called out, "And give us a blanket."

"A blanket?" the boy said. "*My* blanket?"

"That will do. Long as you brush off the spiders."

Lance nudged the others and jerked his head toward the open stable door. The predawn light revealed a world in shades of gray. Soon it would be sunrise. They had to leave now or risk missing the ferry.

He slipped on his knapsack, taking care to silence the treacherous purse. Rayva and MrsKeller gathered their belongings too. They waited for the stable boy to get his blanket and for Duncan to settle down.

Soon it was quiet except for Duncan's snores.

Lance unlatched the gate, stepped out, and nearly collided with the stable boy.

The boy's mouth hung open, a perfect "O" of astonishment.

MrsKeller spoke up. "Paying customers," he explained. "In a bit of a hurry." He bolted through the door, with Lance and Rayva at his heels.

They ran past the Pig and Whistle. Its doors were still open for business if anyone was brave enough to wake the barkeep, who was stretched out along the counter. The few remaining customers were not likely to require service. All were asleep on the tables.

There was no need to trouble anyone for directions. Beck said they'd find Seagate at the northern tip of Liander, just east of Castle Ruinos. All they had to do was keep in line with the castle's crenellated watchtowers.

They headed north on Castle Street, which was wide and cobbled and divided the Royal District neatly in two. Running here was out of the question: they'd attract attention and might be arrested on suspicion of being thieves. Instead they pretended to be sightseers, casually taking in the wonders of the big city.

The Royal District was reserved for Liander's wealthiest citizens. It was entirely residential, and the stone mansions were set well back from the road, with formal gardens in the front. The gardeners were out early, pruning topiary, securing espaliered fruit trees, and mulching the flower beds for winter. Household slaves were busy sweeping the walks and scrubbing steps, and dairy maids carried buckets of sheep and goat's milk or baskets of fresh cheese. Occasionally a worker might look at them with mild curiosity, but no one cared enough to greet or question them.

Rayva kept turning around to see if they were being followed. She grew increasingly nervous as they approached the castle. She was terrified of being questioned by soldiers or guards, certain that someone would discover her secret. At the end of the road, however, there were no soldiers. There was nothing but a black granite wall that stretched far to the east and west as far as the eye could see, and was high enough to hide the castle from people on the road.

The area in front of the wall was deserted, but Rayva felt many eyes spying on them through well-placed cracks and peepholes. She was certain that someone noted their every step: from the end of Castle Road to the wide, gabled arch of Seagate.

Rayva could barely contain her impatience, and she ran as soon as she noticed a break in the wall. She saw a wide archway, closed off by an iron gate. Through the bars she saw a dock and a stretch of water. Across the water was a long coastline. It seemed to be almost within swimming distance.

Lance eyed the view doubtfully. He pointed to a wooded round of land projecting into the sea. "Is that the Weald?" he asked in a low voice. "It looks like an island."

"It's not," she said. "I'm positive. Beck told me that from the ferry dock, the Weald seems like an island, but it's actually connected to the Northern Lands. It's a natural landbridge—an isthmus. You can only see it if you go to the north side of the Weald."

Rayva tried to slide the gate open, but it wouldn't budge. "Locked!" she said. "Or is it jammed?" She rattled the iron bars with both hands.

Suddenly a guard appeared on the other side of the gate. He wore a round, bowl-shaped helmet and a tabard emblazoned with an image of Castle Ruinos.

"What's the racket about, girl?"

Rayva cleared her throat nervously. "I thought the gate might be stuck."

The guard seemed to find this amusing. "It's stuck all right."

"Could you open it for us?" Rayva tried to be polite, though she was sure that the guard was being deliberatrely unhelpful. "We'd like to wait on the dock."

The soldier jerked his thumb toward the road. "Take a hike, sister. There's no ferry here."

"Isn't this Seagate—where the ferry stops?"

"Yeah, but the ferry's not for you. Soldiers and masons only—Lady Alchemia's orders."

Lance saw the color drain from Rayva's face. He stepped forward quickly. "What if we want to take a little boat ride?" He untied his purse and tossed it gently from hand to hand. "It's a nice day for it."

"Nice day?" The guard stared hungrily at the jingling sack. "That depends. People who try for the Northern Lands without her ladyship's permission may get caught in bad weather."

Rayva wondered if the guard meant that literally.

"We don't mind a little rain," Lance said. "We just need a boat."

The guard gestured to the T-shaped pier. "The only thing left is Old Tamas's coracle. It's not mine to sell, but I could loan it to you."

Lance squinted at an odd little craft that bobbed up and

down, secured to a pole. "That looks like a basket. It can't hold three of us."

The guard's eyes opened wide in mock astonishment. "To be sure it can. It's made of Fashe Island reeds: completely watertight."

Lance looked doubtful, but what choice did they have? He offered five pieces of silver.

"Five? You must be joking," the guard parried. "Especially since the only other choice is a long, cold swim."

"Ten," Lance said.

The guard only laughed at him. "Try thirty."

Lance opened his purse and scrutinized the contents. "Twenty-five," he agreed. "And that's final."

"Done!" The guard pocketed the money and unlocked the gate. "Follow me."

They crossed the length of the wooden pier. It was low tide, and the sea was in retreat. Barnacle-covered rocks lay exposed on the sea floor, surrounded by heaps of sea grape and kelp. Starfish and crabs, caught in the tangles, rotted in the sun.

The water seemed deep at the end of the pier, and up close the coracle looked even flimsier. It was shaped like a squat canoe. There were four paddles inside.

They climbed in gingerly. The soldier unlooped the boat from its mooring, unhooked the oars, and shoved them away from the dock with his foot.

"Have a nice trip," he said, and began to laugh.

They each grabbed a paddle and pulled toward the Weald.

"Somehow I feel like we've just been ripped off," Lance said. "We'll probably see the ferry filled with regular people any minute now."

"No matter," MrsKeller said. "It works out better this way. We can take Rayva straight across to the North."

"You don't mind?" Rayva wanted to shout with joy.

"We had planned to do that anyway," Lance explained. "The only reason to go to the Weald first was because of the ferry."

They decided to land the coracle on an open stretch of shore to the west of the Dark Weald. From there Rayva would head inland. They paddled hard, and Rayva was confident that her feet would be on free soil in less than ten minutes.

The currents, however, were working against them. Instead of heading to the mainland, they were being forced toward the Weald's rocky coastline. They redoubled their efforts, but couldn't change course. The coracle moved unerringly toward the peninsula and a stretch of jagged boulders that jutted from the water like broken teeth.

Overhead, the sky darkened with gathering storm clouds. "Don't like the looks of that," Lance said.

Rayva tried to reply, but her voice was swallowed up by a clap of thunder. In an instant, sea and sky went gray, and rain pelted down. The wind began to howl, and gentle swells turned into whitecaps that rose five and six feet high.

The coracle creaked and groaned as it crested and fell. Water began to seep through the bottom. As the depth of water increased, the reeds split apart. Soon the seep became a gush, and the unsinkable Fashe Island vessel went down to the bottom.

They clung to their paddles and gave themselves over to the current. They no longer cared about getting to the mainland: they only thought about getting out of the water. The current swept them to the far side of the peninsula. They saw the isthmus: it was covered with tents. And on the northern tip of the Weald, a hundred slaves were laboring in the rain, dragging huge stones up a ramp to a half-built wall.

They could scarcely take it in. A moment later, they lost sight of land altogether. An enormous wall of water rose up and crashed over them, and then they were separated. Lance was cut off, isolated in the violent peaks and valleys of water.

He screamed, "Adam! Rayva!" Then another wave swept him up and rolled him under.

Rayva thought she heard him shout, but she couldn't see him anywhere. She called his name and treaded water, churning her legs to boost herself up a few inches. She had one frightening view of emptiness, and a wave slapped her across the face and blinded her. Icy water closed over her head. Her long cloak and robe became heavy weights that dragged her down into blackness. The cold and dark confused her. She didn't know if she was swimming toward the bottom or the surface.

Suddenly she felt her arm wrenched upward. She thought wildly of monsters and sharks, then realized it was human fingers gripping her wrist—fingers that must belong to one of her companions. She kicked her legs to propel them both forward. In a violent burst, she and MrsKeller broke the surface of the water.

MrsKeller choked out a few words, but Rayva only understood one: "*Lance.*"

She pointed to the area where she had heard him. They scanned the surface of the waves with red, salt-stung eyes, but saw nothing until they looked toward the shore. Lance was standing at the waterline holding a wet rabbit in one hand and waving with the other.

Chapter Twenty-Two

R ayva and MrsKeller dragged themselves to the beach
and rejoined Lance. For a few moments they sat shivering, too exhausted to move. The storm was dying down, but
there were still signs of it everywhere: the waves continued to
explode against the rocky ledges to the north, and the sandy
shore was white with foam. The rabbit sat in Lance's lap, its
long ears snapping in the wind like pennants.

"Should he be out?" MrsKeller said. He seemed to be avoiding Rayva's eyes.

"My pack's gone," Lance answered. "Where can I hide him?"

"Your shirt?" suggested MrsKeller.

Lance shrugged. "Can't think of a better place. If I keep my
cloak on, no one should notice." He dropped the rabbit down
the front of his tunic. It settled in a fold above his belt.

Rayva kept her eyes fixed on the sand. Her cheeks were wet
with tears or spray, and her black hair circled her neck like a
noose.

Lance carefully unwound it and slipped his arm around
her shoulders. "We're not that far from the North," he said. "We

can swim to the coast once the storm is over."

"Sure. And look"—MrsKeller waved his hand to the sky—"the weather's improving already."

It was true. The sun was shining through a ragged hole in the clouds, and the waves sparkled with dancing motes of light.

"It won't last." Rayva's voice was bleak. "We're not allowed north. As soon as we go into the sea, Alchemia will make make it happen again. The guard warned us."

Lance wrapped both arms around her and held her tight for one brief moment. "Don't worry, Rave. We'll figure it out."

She leaned against him wearily. "I don't see how."

He looked over the top of her head and met MrsKeller's eyes. "We're meeting somebody here who might be able to help you. He shouldn't be far away."

They got up and started walking, and she followed apathetically. They found a road near the coast and moved along it in silence. The boys seemed to know where they were headed.

Rayva listened to the white pines creaking in the wind. The road turned inland, to a clearing in the woods with a tall, black • stone in the center. No one was waiting for them.

Rayva sank down at the foot of a bare maple tree. The fallen leaves were still crimson, pooled around the trunk like blood. Without meaning to she sighed aloud. "We're all prisoners in Discordia."

The boys stared at her. They seemed frightened.

"What's the matter?" she asked. "What did I say?"

"Repeat that—please." Lance's voice sounded thin and strange.

"We're all prisoners?"

"That other word."

"Discordia?" She was confused. "I don't even know what it means—it just popped into my head."

The boys began to speak to each other in low, quick voices.

"She's a gamer—got to be," MrsKeller said.

Lance was nodding. "Maybe TheGreatOne brought her here too."

"Of *course* he did."

"We'll take her back. . . ." Lance paused. "If we can."

Rayva looked from one to the other in total bewilderment. "What do you mean—take me back to what?"

"*Our* world," MrsKeller said. He was serious, even solemn. "Yours, mine, and Lance's. *That's* your home—not here."

How could one small word be proof of that? She shook her head emphatically. "You're making too much of this—leaping to conclusions. . . ."

Lance stretched out his hand and touched her shoulder. "It's true," he said. "Discordia is a game from our world, but it's modeled after this one: the topography, the politics, the monsters—MrsKeller and I used to play it together." He looked chagrined. "On the Perdition side."

Rayva stared him him in disbelief. "A game?"

"Yes," said MrsKeller. "And we were actually *in* Discordia as we played. Lance played a zombie sorcerer, and I was a hobgoblin brigand."

Rayva's teeth began to chatter. "How could you play at such a thing? It makes no sense."

"It would take too long to explain," Lance said. "I'm afraid you'll freeze to death if we go into it now. The important thing is, someone brought us here for a quest, and he's supposed to meet us. He wants us to destroy Alchemia's wand, and if we do that, he'll show us how to get home." Lance looked at her earnestly. "Do you understand?"

"Not a thing," she said. "You actually think you can get Alchemia's wand?"

Lance pulled her to her feet. "Never mind," he said. "You're coming with us. What do you have to lose?"

"Where are you going?" She gestured at the empty clearing. "You still expect your friend to arrive?"

"Not here," he told her. "He said this might happen, and he's given us a backup plan. If it works, we'll escape. If it doesn't, we'll try a different plan. If that fails too, we'll be stuck here together." He paused expectantly. "So what do you say? Want to give it a shot?"

She thought for a moment. What *did* she have to lose? Anywhere was safer than the Weald. "You really believe there's a way out?"

"Yep," MrsKeller said. "And it all starts in Wealock Prison. I'll fill you in while we walk."

They went back to the road and continued on. Rayva felt as if she were in a dream as she listened to MrsKeller's description of a portal that would lead to another world. One portal door might be in the prison dungeon; the other might be in Alchemia's workshop. If they had a choice, they'd try for the least dangerous of the two, but they couldn't know the details until they showed up at the prison's kitchen, where their quest was supposed to begin.

MrsKeller thought Rayva should join them, saying that she

had come there hoping for a job. She and Lance disagreed. It was better to be cautious at first. She'd wait for them to assess the situation. As soon as they could get away, they'd discuss the next step together.

Rayva's spirits were rising. They had discovered a good place for her to hide within view of the prison: in a small copse of fir trees. The thick branches would provide cover and a modicum of shelter, and she'd be close at hand if they needed to get her quickly.

Everything felt hopeful until it was time for the boys to leave. She realized that she would be alone soon, staring at the low, slate-gray building and its single tower. The sight oppressed her. "I wish you didn't have to do this."

"We have to try," Lance said. "If we're expected in the kitchen, everything should go well."

Rayva twisted her fingers together to stop herself from grabbing his arm. "Good luck, then. I'll be waiting."

Lance gave her a little hug. "See you soon."

He squared his shoulders. "Ready, Adam?"

"As I'll ever be."

They set off for the kitchen.

Chapter Twenty-Three

T he kitchen was located in the rear of the building. Its six chimneys were wreathed in smoke, and the great double doors were thrown open to let out the heat. From their vantage point, the boys saw a long section of open hearth and brick, a beehive oven with a gaping door. A man with a beard that covered his chest was pulling out flat, round loaves with a long-handled wooden paddle and tossing them into a woven basket on the floor.

A few others raced back and forth, intent on other chores. They all wore drab, floor-length tunics and dirty bib aprons. A small woman stood in the center of the room, barking commands.

She spoke to an unseen worker to the left of the doorway. "Earth and sky, Erin! You'll upset the entire cauldron that way. Finish up already and help with the slicing. There are three whole roasts here and not one has been touched."

Then she glanced out the door and saw the boys. She waved them in. "It's about time," she said. "They've been promising us extra help for days."

MrsKeller gave her a big grin and sprang forward. He completed his entrance with a flourish, taking a theatrical gasp when he crossed the threshold.

Lance thought this was a bit overdone. He entered more sedately, but in a moment he nearly cried out—he couldn't help it. When he crossed the threshold he felt the cold metal close around his neck.

The woman made a loud, disapproving sniff. "Welcome to Wealock Prison," she said. "Soon to be known as Fort Wealock. I'm Arlette, your forewoman. At the moment I'm also head cook by default. This lot can't distinguish between a rag and a *ragu.*"

She waited for them to respond, or even to smile, but they stayed where they were, mute and motionless. She threw up her hands. "They promise a new crew from the city, and all we get are two daft kitchen slaves—imbeciles, from the looks of them."

"Go easy on the poor lads," the baker protested. "They're not volunteers."

"Who is, I'd like to know?" The forewoman picked up a carving knife and attacked a roast. "New boys," she said, "pots!"

They didn't move fast enough, so she grabbed their sleeves and led them to a stone basin.

"There are your scrubbing brushes, there are the pots—" She tilted her chin in the air and yelled, "Rose, hot water!"

A woman rushed in with a heavy bucket. Tendrils of curls had escaped her scarf, and her pink cheeks were damp with steam.

"And there," Arlette continued, "is your hot water."

With a grunt, the woman tipped the water into the sink, then set it on the floor with a heavy *thunk*. She fanned her face with one hand, displaying one of the brawniest forearms that Lance had ever seen.

"Rough crossing?" she asked with a friendly smile. "Storms are getting fierce—"

Arlette marched over and prodded Rose with an empty basket. "You're gabbing when you ought to be helping with the trenchers."

"Yes, Arlette." Rose walked off, but as soon as Arlette returned to her carving, she doubled back to the sink. She stooped over the murky water, pretending to hunt for a utensil.

"Don't be so gloomy," she said out of the corner of her mouth. "I'd heard the same stories before I got here, but I've never seen a single ghost—not one. Ellen claims she's heard them moving round in the main hall, but she's high-strung— jumps at every shadow."

Lance tried to keep his voice steady. "What did she say they looked like?"

Rose looked up in surprise. "She didn't *see* them. We're not allowed in the main hall. No one is but Lady Alchemia. Didn't they tell you that on the ferry?"

Lance shrugged. "Maybe they were too busy—with the storm and all."

"Of course! Don't worry. I'll fill you in later." She shook the water from her hands and picked up the basket.

"Is the lady here often?" MrsKeller asked.

Rose checked to see if Arlette was watching. "Never seen her myself," she whispered. "They say she's up in the workshop sometimes, but there's no sleeping quarters for her yet—not until they finish building."

Lance accidentally let the scrubbing brush slip through his fingers. Arlette heard and set her knife on the table.

"Rose," she said in an awful voice, "there's a battalion of Warriors out there. If you keep them waiting, you'll end up dead as mutton."

She turned to Lance and MrsKeller. "The same goes for you, new boys." She pointed to a stack of empty buckets. "Put down that washing and get me four full buckets. The well is to the left of the fir trees—and make it quick."

MrsKeller was already out the door with a bucket in each hand. Lance gathered the others and went after him.

"Adam—" He was afraid to raise his voice. "Adam!"

MrsKeller spun around. "It's still *on*." His neck bulged over the metal band. "I thought it might disappear when we got outside."

Lance felt sick. How would they tell Rayva that they were slaves now?

He saw the well and dumped the buckets on the ground before he plunged through the fir trees.

"Rayva?" he called, trying to keep from shouting.

She had been curled into a little ball under her wet cloak, but jumped up when she heard his voice.

MrsKeller saw the movement and ran toward her. His fingers clawed at his neck. "Look at this!" he gasped. "Is it fake? Can you tell?"

She covered her mouth with her hands.

"I have one too," Lance said.

Her eyes moved from one collar to the other. "What happened?" she whispered.

"Don't know," Lance said. "We walked into the kitchen and felt them on our necks."

Rayva tried to make sense of what she was seeing. "So no one put them on you? No Warriors?"

"No," Lance said quickly. He saw her face clear a little. "Is that a good sign?"

"Maybe," she said. "Oh, I hope so. Everyone I know had their collars locked on by the Warriors. It's always done that way."

Lance was breathing rapidly. "Maybe these *are* fake," he said. "It might be some kind of magic to help us blend in with the kitchen crew."

"It must be," she said. "You can't be slaves. You can't."

"But what if we are?" MrsKeller asked. "Maybe our memories will be wiped out like yours."

She grabbed his shoulder and shook him fiercely. "If you forget who you are, I'll remind you. But you should start looking for a way out tonight."

"Tonight?" MrsKeller thought about this for a moment. "I guess the collars won't make any difference. But if we get caught—"

"Then it won't matter anyway," she said firmly. "Come get me when everyone's sleeping, or sooner if it seems safe. I'll stay where I am."

"I hate to leave you out here alone," Lance said. "And you must be frozen solid."

She tried to smile. "It's not so bad. With all this wind, my cloak is practically dry."

"I wish I could give you mine," Lance said.

"Don't worry about me. It's much more important that we hide the bunya." She gave them each a quick hug, then shoved them away. "Better get back or you'll be in trouble. See you later."

They filled the buckets and hurried back to the kitchen. As soon as they came in, Arlette began to scold.

"I don't know how it was for you before, but here we take care of six dozen troops. There's no time to waste, and likely enough it will only get worse."

She set them to work immediately, and for the rest of the afternoon they toiled with the others. It was dark outside when the last pot had been washed and put away. The slaves drifted out of the kitchen and into the hall where they slept; Lance and MrsKeller stayed behind as if too exhausted to move.

MrsKeller sat on the floor and leaned his head against the wall. He closed his eyes and pretended to be dozing, but one hand had disappeared beneath the sink. Out of the corner of his mouth he whispered, "It's here. Box of stuff."

Lance heard little clinks of metal and wood, but then Arlette appeared in the doorway, and MrsKeller's rummaging ceased immediately.

"Don't stay here," she said. "We go to the sleeping quarters now."

They followed her into the narrow corridor. Flaming torches lined the walls and cast a feeble glow over eight straw mattresses that were lined up against one wall. All but three were occupied.

Arlette pointed to the two that were farthest away from the kitchen. "These are yours," she said. "You have the least seniority, so you're closest to the doorway."

"Doorway to what?" Lance said.

Arlette's lips formed a thin line. "The prison, of course. It's locked." She turned on her heel and walked to her own mattress. Lance noticed that it was the one closest to the kitchen.

The baker caught their eye and gestured them over. "Before you lads came, I was the one near the door, and believe me, I would have been happy if the door had been locked and barred twelve times."

Lance hoped they could keep him talking. "Did you see any ghosts? Someone told us they'd heard strange sounds in the main hall."

The baker grimaced. "That's what's on the other side of this door: the main hall. As for ghosts, that might be the least of our worries."

MrsKeller clutched his arm. "What do you mean? Something worse?"

"Let's just say that I was here when the porter slaves arrived carrying people on stretchers into the main hall, and not a single one of them was too healthy." He tapped the side of his nose, but the boys didn't understand what this was supposed to mean.

"Why were they here, then?" Lance asked. "Was this some kind of hospital?"

The baker gave a short bark of laughter. "Hospital, lad? That's for the living." After a long pause he muttered, "We could smell the poor sods back here, in the kitchen."

"But why were they here?" Lance asked.

The baker turned ever so slightly toward the heavy door. "Only Lady Alchemia knows the answer to that question, and I ain't asking." He jerked his thick forefinger toward the ceiling. "Up and down the stairs the porter slaves were. The stretchers went up there too, and so did her ladyship." He bent toward them. "Her ladyship, she's not been around lately"—he lowered his voice to a hoarse whisper—"but them things on the stretchers never left."

"You three down there—enough chatter," Arlette shouted. "In a few hours we have to be back in the kitchen, and if anyone disturbs my rest . . ." She didn't bother finishing the sentence.

Without another word they went to their thin mattresses. Lance unfolded the blanket they had left for him. He spread it over himself and lay down on his side, careful not to crush the rabbit.

He listened for noises on the other side of the metal door, but it seemed perfectly quiet. The only sounds were from the other slaves as they shifted restlessly on their hard beds or murmured to each other. After a long while, the slaves settled into their dreams. It was time to try the kitchen.

He tapped MrsKeller's shoulder. They both rose as stealthily as possible and tiptoed past the other mattresses. They entered the kitchen quietly. The only light came from the glowing embers in the fireplaces, but it was just enough for MrsKeller to locate the box below the sink. He tucked it under one arm while Lance gently lifted the iron latch of the double door. He pushed one door just wide enough, and they slipped out into the night.

Chapter Twenty-four

The crescent moon was an insignificant sliver of light in a sky pierced by dazzling stars. To the east was a somber patch of purple gray. Could it be dawn already? They raced to the stand of fir trees.

Rayva was already waiting for them. She must have been too anxious to sleep. Lance started to greet her, but the sound was cut short by a callused hand. He lurched to the left, using his full weight to break free. The dagger point at his ear convinced him to stop. He straightened slowly as the point traced a line to the base of his jaw.

A deep male voice said, "You lads have kept Rayva waiting for quite some time."

Lance felt a rope tighten around his wrists, and heard a clatter of metal followed by a woman's laughter. "Stars above, the lad's armed!"

"Tied his hands yet?"

"Of course." A woman with short white-blond hair shoved MrsKeller next to Lance and Rayva.

The attackers stood in front of them. Both were brigands,

similarly dressed in brown hose, thick leather boots, and short brown tunics heavily padded and covered with chain mail. Neither wore a cloak, as it would have hindered access to their weapons. Leather straps crisscrossed their chests to hold daggers and small throwing knives, and long blades hung in scabbards from their belts.

"What was he carrying, then?" the man asked.

"A ladle, my dear, and some slotted spoons."

"Kitchen tools?" He gave a low, respectful whistle as he untied Rayva's gag. "That's dangerous, that is."

As soon as the cloth was loosened, Rayva spat out, "These are the idiots who grabbed me in the alley, and here they are again." She faced them squarely. "I don't get it. I had nothing to give you in Liander, and I have nothing to give you here."

"Nothing?" The woman poked at Lance's neck. "How about information worth fifty bags of gold."

"We don't know anything," Rayva said.

The brigand laughed. "Hear that, Neil? She sounds so convincing: a real artist. Good enough to fool lots of folks—"

Neil snorted, "Like that blockhead Duncan."

"But not us," Whimsey said. "Though I admit, I'm truly impressed—and I used to be an espionage rogue, so that's saying something."

"Makes you think, doesn't it, Whim?"

The woman nodded. "The druids must be coming up with some new ideas." She jerked her chin at Lance. "He does the corpse monster one day, fakes a slave collar the next. I wish we had time to see how it's done."

Lance glared at her. "I don't know what you're talking about."

"Never mind," she said. "After you lead us to the Penance command post, and we finish rounding up whoever's inside, Neil and I will find a way to convince you."

"You think there's a command post here?" Lance stuttered. "Are you crazy?"

Whimsey gave him a push and began to herd them in a wide arc around the kitchen. "Like a fox, slave boy. Crazy like a fox."

The brigands laughed softly.

"Nice try, Lance, but it's too late to play innocent. Me and Whim have been on your tail every step of the way: from the toll road to Liander, to the guild house, to the Pig and Whistle—"

"And the stable too," Whimsey said with a hint of professional pride. She stifled a yawn and prodded Lance between his shoulder blades. "Long job—I have to say—but interesting."

"Not nearly as interesting as it *will* be," Neil added. "The real fun starts when we find those portals."

"Portals?" MrsKeller turned his head sharply, dreads whipping Lance across the face. "What's that?"

The startled, incredulous act was well done, but the brigands didn't buy it.

"Oh—*you* know," Neil said. "Of course you do. *Portals.*" He emphasized the word with a shove. "The ones that take you to the North—the place you lads call 'home.'"

"Portals to the North," Whimsey said in a dreamy tone. "And from what we've overheard, they're right here under the Lady's nose." She jangled her coin purse, making the metal ring. "That's what I call valuable information."

Lance shook his head. It was all wrong, but why argue? They'd see for themselves soon enough, and they wouldn't be happy. Still, they'd collect the bounty for three Penance spies. That would be some consolation.

"All right, lads and lady, we're off to the main hall," Neil said jovially.

The main hall? Not the garrison? Lance's mind was racing. The brigands must be here in secret, wanting all the credit and glory for themselves. That meant they'd have no backup—didn't expect to need any.

Lance could hardly wait to see their expressions when they came face-to-face with TheGreatOne. If he was there. TheGreatOne hadn't fulfilled his part of the plan at all. Lance had a sinking feeling that they'd seen the last of him.

The brigands urged them on with the edge of their daggers. As they neared the prison, they grew increasingly vigilant, on the lookout for soldiers.

"Not another word from any of you," Whimsey said, but the warning was unnecessary. Who would help them now?

Rayva and MrsKeller were making a final, desperate effort, trying to wriggle their arms free with small, furtive movements. Lance didn't bother. He remembered how it had been with Duncan. The more he'd struggled, the worse it had been. The ropes bit into his flesh and the knots held firm. Duncan had laughed at him. But then the zombie emerged: a dormant predator awakened by the thought of blood.

Should he try to get the zombie back? Last time it had saved them, but that had been an accident. This time, it might attack—go after his friends first. Unlike the brigands, Rayva and MrsKeller were unarmed, defenseless. If the zombie devoured them, he would be a murderer: he and the zombie were one.

He wished he could summon the monster and control it, yet he had no confidence in his powers. The savage hunger would take and obliterate him forever. They'd all be lost. And yet—

Lance knew that he'd have to try: summon the beast, call on the monster within. And he'd have to be stronger than the zombie. It was their only chance.

They were almost in view of the main hall. Lance struggled against the ropes, hoping that the zombie would emerge. This time he couldn't detect the slightest hint of the other being.

He closed his eyes and thought of the Mara and then the strangleworm, but the images left him cold. He pictured raw meat oozing blood on a marble slab, an opened vein, a crimson tube running from a donor's arm into a slowly filling plastic sack. Nothing happened. He was weak, useless, unchanged.

The brigands forced him up the steps to an iron door. Whimsey pushed against the latch, and it slowly swung outward. Lance and his friends were jostled inside. The brigands unhooked squat, glass-sided lanterns from their belts. Neil used a tinderbox to light the wicks, and the room jumped into focus.

There were three iron cages on either side of the doorway, identical to the ones in the game, except these were empty. The light from the oil lamps was too feeble to reach the corners of the room, but it did reveal the two shadowy archways opposite the door.

Neil turned right until Whimsey called him back.

"That's the staircase, blockhead—to the lady's workshop."

"Oh, right," he said. "They won't be meeting up there."

The brigands began to herd their prisoners down a sloping hallway. The lanterns scarcely lifted the gloom.

Lance felt suffocated by the dark. He recalled the dungeon

creatures in the game and the treacherous winding ramps and remembered how the adrenaline surged through his body. He used to laugh at himself for being frightened. Until he entered Discordia, he had never been truly frightened. Now he knew the difference.

They reached a door. Whimsey knocked. "In there, Penance pals? We know you are." She shook her hand vigorously. "That smarts," she said. "The door must be solid iron." She grabbed the latch, but the door wouldn't budge.

Neil set his lamp on the floor and pressed his ear to the surface. "Hang on!" he said. "I hear something moving on the other side."

Lance heard it too: a slow, scraping sound. He and MrsKeller exchanged terrified looks. "Don't open the door," he said. "It's not what you think in there—nothing to do with Penance at all."

"Good one," Neil said. He and Whimsey continued their assault on the door.

"I'm telling the truth!" Lance's voice was urgent. "Alchemia has creatures in there—and they're locked away for a reason—"

The brigands gave the door one final push. It swung inward with a rusty groan. Neil picked up his lamp and poked his head inside. "Huh," he said. "It stinks in here." He knelt down to shine the light along the floor. "Something must have died—"

Someone knocked the lamp from his hand. Neil drew a dagger and slashed at his attacker. It was a direct hit. The dagger sank through skin and muscle, and then there was a sodden pop and the resistance was gone.

This was all wrong. He would have sworn that he had cut through flesh—perhaps a limb. He had sliced through dozens of arms, but none like this. The texture was wrong—too yielding—

and even the sound was peculiar. Also there was no scream.

He turned to his partner. "What did I just cut?"

"Couldn't see a thing," Whimsey said. She squatted down next to him. "Heard it, though." She set Neil's lamp right side up and held hers at arm's length.

"See anything?" he asked.

"No . . ." She paused and squinted into the dark. "Hang on." Her voice dropped to a whisper. "I see it."

"Get out while you can," Lance yelled. "There could be zombies inside."

Rayva shrieked with alarm, but Whimsey only laughed.

"I suppose you know best, monster boy."

Whimsey crawled forward a few inches and let out a scream. Her lantern rolled onto its side. The oil was leaking out, and the flame still burned. Neil rushed to her side.

For a moment the three captives looked on with huge, terrified eyes. Then they began to tiptoe backward, trying to keep their movements quiet. As they increased their distance from the open door, they went faster and made more noise. Halfway up the corridor, they turned around and ran.

The brigands had forgotten them. Whimsey was still rolling on the floor, screaming and wrestling with shadows. Neil struck out at the space around her body. His weapons sliced through the air, unimpeded.

"Whim," he shouted. "Stop—you're all right. Nothing's there."

"Yes! Strangling!" She shook her head violently. "Help me!"

She seemed to have lost her mind. Neil tried to lift her from the floor and carry her away but stopped when he saw something move. He squinted into the dark. A man was crawling toward them. The light was so bad that Neil could only distinguish the arm in a ragged sleeve.

He straightened up and stamped on it. The arm squelched beneath his boot—a shockingly unexpected sensation. He lifted his foot to examine it, and the arm came with it, stuck to the sole.

Neil began to laugh. How had he let himself get so scared? There was no ragged person sneaking up on them—only a stinking severed arm with skin hanging in tatters—left there to rot.

So this was the culprit? Neil kept laughing. He roared at his partner and told her to get a grip, but she continued to roll on the floor, clutching her neck.

"Snap out of it," he said.

He grabbed the fetid limb by the wrist and waved it in her face. The dangling hand grabbed back.

He tried to shake it off, but it hung on tenaciously. He smashed it against the wall, screeching with horror and pain. The hand squeezed tighter.

He tried to break the hold with his boot, but when he lifted his foot he discovered two more hands—one large, one small—crawling up his leg like spiders. He hurled himself to the floor, trying to crush them with his body. They kept moving. They seemed to be everywhere, drawn to the flickering light of their oil lamps. Severed hands and feet moved rapidly, bending and flexing their joints. Bits of torso and thigh were dragged by ribbons of skin that crept across the floor like inchworms dragging a bone.

The body parts surged toward the living, forming putrid piles. Soon they had muffled the screams and stilled the tortured convulsions. Silently, they dragged the corpses into the dark.

chapter twenty-five

L ance, Rayva, and MrsKeller lurched up the passageway, arms bound behind their backs. They were panting
hard and straining their eyes for a glimpse of the main hall.
When they reached it, the front door was still open. A crack of
light was shining through.

Lance wanted to run outside into the open air, but they had
to look for the portal. MrsKeller was already heading for the
tower, and Rayva was right behind him. Without hesitating,
she bounded up the stairs. Lance followed.

The circular staircase was freestanding and wound its way
to the top, where narrow rectangular windows threw thin
beams of light along the steps. Lance glanced up at the windows, and immediately wished he hadn't. A wave of vertigo
swept over him, forcing him to stop and lean against the wall.
He closed his eyes, but that made it worse, as though the stairs
were slanting away, forcing him to slide downward.

He stared at the central shaft and took a few deep breaths to
steady himself. Drops of sweat stung his eyes, but he couldn't
blink them away. His hands felt cold and numb, and they

tingled unpleasantly. He tried to think of nothing but the portal. His friends might be staring at it right now, ready to step through. He forced himself to go on, step by step, until he reached the landing.

With a sigh of relief he walked into the room. It was lined with large windows. A skylight overhead illuminated a polished oak table. One side of the table was covered with dark baskets filled with dried herbs; the other side with small glass bottles. There was a hint of rosemary in the air, and it was very quiet.

Lance was still breathing hard, and he felt odd—almost detached. He wondered if he was still affected by the vertigo. His mind was nearly blank, yet he felt drawn to something on the table.

He drew closer. In the center of the table he saw a casket about as long as his arm, made of translucent gems as green and blue as a tropical sea. He had to touch it. Without thinking he broke through the bonds at his wrist, and the ropes fell to the floor. Slowly he lifted the lid. On a black velvet cushion was a wand: slender, translucent, and cobalt blue. He lifted it from the velvet.

There was a rustle behind him. Lance turned and looked up at The GreatOne. His eye sockets glowed red.

"Congratulations," he said. "You have found the Primo: Alchemia's Doom."

"We didn't think you would come." Lance ducked to the side, trying to spot his friends. "Where's MrsKeller and Rayva?"

"They're here, of course." The zombie chuckled. "But they're a little tied up at the moment. You know: busy."

Tied up? It suddenly occurred to Lance that he had been tied up also. He wasn't anymore.

He dashed around the corner and saw Rayva and Adam

sitting knees to their chests, bound to the wall with hundreds of silver strands.

They stared straight ahead, as senseless as if they were made of wax.

"What have you done with them?"

"I?" The zombie sounded surprised. "Nothing! They've gotten caught in the Strands of Tarsa, a little trap invented by the same lady who came up with the egg slicer. They tried to get the wand, and they got caught."

Lance ran his fingers over the wire, testing it for weakness. "Can't you get them out of here?"

"Alas"—the zombie wrung his hands—"my own powers are not sufficient—though perhaps with the help of that wand . . ."

Desperate to get his friends out, Lance was about to hand the wand over, yet something made him hesitate. "You know how it works."

The zombie reached for it. "I can but try."

Lance pulled back. "Why'd they get caught and not me?"

"Who knows?" TheGreatOne said airily. "Best to not get bogged down in trivialities at such a crucial time."

Lance noticed that the zombie's eyes were pulsing. It made him look shifty, like someone making up a lie as he went along.

The zombie gestured at the wall. "Those little silver threads—thin as piano wire but ten times as strong? In about two minutes they'll slice your pals into neat little slices." After every word, the zombie moved a little bit closer.

Lance pushed against the zombie's rib cage and shoved him away. "You're lying—"

"I am not!" TheGreatOne said, deeply offended. "We've

grouped together for this quest. We're *guild mates*. We work together for a common goal."

"Really? *Our* goal is to go home, so maybe we should compromise. If you let go of my friends and tell me how to get out of here, then you can have the wand."

The zombie waggled a finger at him. "Wand first, Lance. Can't do a thing without it."

"Wait a minute," Lance said. "You just said you weren't sure you could use it at all."

TheGreatOne paused. "Actually, I *was* lying. The Tarsa is my invention. Alkie doesn't have enough style for that sort of thing." The zombie extended a hand. "You really should stop stalling. It won't do you any good to wait, and it certainly won't help your friends."

Lance looked at his friends' blank faces. He would give the wand away without a second thought if he trusted the zombie, but he didn't. *He couldn't.*

"Why didn't you just take the wand yourself," he said. "Why did you need us at all?"

The zombie clasped his hands together. "If only I could have! But Alchemia created a wand that would never allow a zombie to lift it from its case. I needed a human to take it out for me. Because once it's out of the box, there's no problem at all."

Lance was edging around the table, trying to keep distance between them. "Why didn't you just ask them?" He kept his eyes fixed on the zombie. "They would have done it, if it meant going home."

"I wasn't at all sure of that, so I figured we'd engage in a little friendly trade—your friends for my wand." As if suddenly inspired, the zombie started to sing.

"Zombies . . . zombies who need people . . . are the luckiest zombies . . . in the world."

The zombie sprang forward and grabbed the wand between his bony fingers.

"Let go," he commanded. "Discordia needs me!"

Lance fought back. "Discordia needs *you*? You're crazier than Alchemia."

"False." The zombie sent a burst of power through the wand, turning it hot as a live coal. "I am TheGreatOne."

Lance's skin blistered in the heat. He screamed with pain, but he wouldn't let go.

"Don't be stubborn, Lance," the zombie said in a concerned voice. "I could boil your blood into vapor, you know, and your friends will still be sliced and diced."

Lance stared defiantly into the glowing red eyes, and the zombie within him roared.

TheGreatOne was oblivious. "You will never defeat me, Lance. You're a zombie slave. I'm a zombie sorcerer."

The zombie within Lance gathered its power and snapped the wand in two. At the same moment, TheGreatOne staggered backward and crashed to the floor. The zombie stepped on the skeleton and turned to the living creatures tied to the wall. He allowed Lance to share the eyes, and he allowed Lance to use the brain. Together, Lance and the zombie ran to his friends and ripped at the Strands of Tarsa. Silver threads flew into the air. Rayva and MrsKeller jumped to their feet. The zombie retreated.

MrsKeller gestured wildly at something on the wall. "It's there—the portal!"

Lance looked to the left of the workshop door. A second door had appeared; at eye height there was a shimmering circle. MrsKeller touched it: his hand disappeared to the wrist.

Lance shoved the fragment of wand into his belt and grabbed Rayva's hand. They ran to MrsKeller, held on to each other, and jumped into the blue. They held on tight, but in the sliver of time between one world and the other, they were separated.

Lance was pulled into the vortex first, and MrsKeller followed a short distance after. Rayva was the farthest away, still the closest to Discordia. The boys tried to go back to her, but an irresistible force pulled them in the opposite direction.

She tried to move forward, and flailed her arms and legs—swimming with all her might. She was gaining momentum bit by bit, just on the verge of being swept toward the boys. Soon the force would gather her in, and she'd be there beside them. Lance yelled triumphantly. She turned to him and smiled, and at that moment skeletal arms burst into the portal and seized her. Rayva twisted savagely, but the arms dragged her away.

"Rayva!" Lance screamed. "Rayva! We'll come back!"

She was gone. Then MrsKeller was gone, and Lance was in a place without sound, color, or sensation. For a moment he ceased to exist; then he emerged on the other side. He was in the dark of his own room. There was a fragment of cobalt-blue glass in his hand, and a brown-and-white, lop-eared rabbit on his lap.

A message was flashing across his monitor:

"We apologize for the delay. Certain realms have closed due to technical difficulties. Please download the patch again and reenter Discordia."

DISCORDIA

Game Manual continued . . .

FIRST TIME?

If you're new to MMO adventures, you might assume that you'll spend most of your time fighting the opposing faction. That would be wrong. Discordia's *monster* problem is out of control, and it's a major threat to both sides. The creatures come in many varieties. Some are armed, some cast lethal spells, some carry strange and deadly diseases, some are perpetually starved, and some are just plain bloodthirsty. None, however, care about politics. If you cross their paths, you'll be treated as prey, regardless of your race, gender, class, or faction.

You'll run into plenty of hostile nonplayer characters (NPCs) too: human outlaws, mutinous orc and hobgoblin mercenaries, and mutating zombies (from Alchemia's less successful experiments). These NPCs harass both factions and never show favoritism to members of their own race. (Trust us on this: if you've been thinking that an NPC zombie will extend the rotting hand of friendship because you're a fellow zombie, think again.)

MEET THE FACTIONS, PART 1: THE WARRIORS OF PERDITION

If you sign on with Perdition, you'll be fighting to uphold Alchemia's anti-druid, pro-sorcery, gold-loving revolution. The Warriors of Perdition are a mixed-race force. There are humans (Discordia's majority race), orc, and hobgoblin mercenaries from the mountains, and most recently, a battalion of zombies, courtesy of Alchemia's dark arts. (She's perfecting her resurrection techniques at an undisclosed location on the Dark Weald Peninsula.)

Perdition fighters have a bad reputation, which is perfectly understandable. It's hard to stay popular while burning down villages and terrorizing the locals. Still, to their way of thinking, it's better to be the stomper than the stompee.

FAST FACTS

Available races: human, orc, hobgoblin, zombie
Available fighting classes: rogue, brigand, healer, sorcerer, ranger
Commander of the troops: King Lair the Builder
Power behind the throne and Discordia's true ruler: Alchemia Vole, sorcerer
Capital city: Liander

MEET THE FACTIONS, PART 2: THE EXACTERS OF PENANCE

If you sign up with Penance, you won't have to agonize over which race to choose: Penance fighters are all human. (Yes, even the druids.) They're just people who were born with a genetic gift, such as having the potential to run a sub-four-minute mile.

Penance is comprised of many small units known as "cells." Each cell is under the command of a captain. Penance fighters specialize in guerilla warfare, and they take full advantage of their knowledge of the local terrain.

FAST FACTS

Available races: human
Available fighting classes: rogue, brigand, healer, druid, ranger
Commanders of the troops: many
Home turf: the Northern Lands beyond the Dark Weald Peninsula
Capital city: none

WHAT'S A HOBGOBLIN ROGUE GOT THAT I HAVEN'T GOT?

Here's the deal: in Discordia, race matters. Whether you're human, hobgoblin, orc, or zombie, your racial characteristics may influence your choice of class or even your faction, if you want to play a nonhuman character.

Race confers particular advantages and disadvantages to your fighting class. Humans have the edge when it comes to intelligence and dexterity, orcs are great for power and endurance, hobgoblins have speed and agility, and zombies can cannibalize. (By eating a dead enemy, they have the ability to restore health quickly.)

YOU'VE GOT CLASS

Fighting class, that is. Discordian soldiers are separated by specialty, otherwise known as fighting class. Folks in the melee class fight up close and personal. Casters do it with magic. Ranged weapon specialists do it with critters.

Confused? Here's the specifics.

Rogues (melee class) are famous for their stealth; lock-picking and spying abilities; and excellent knife, bow, and sword skills. Their first blows can be crippling, but they can't withstand many counterstrikes: their weak armor limits their durability. Rogues wear cloth armor until level 34, then upgrade to leather.

Brigands (melee class) can dish out the damage (though not as much as rogues), but their real strength is being able to take it. Brigands withstand direct strikes better than any other class in the game, thanks to their excellent armor (chain mail until level 34, then plate armor). In a group, a brigand functions as a living shield (more commonly known as a "tank"). A good tank "holds aggro" by making himself the primary target of an enemy's aggression.

This allows the more vulnerable classes to fight at a safer distance.

Druids (caster class) use magic derived from the forces of nature. They can charm animals, create health-giving potions, and they know how to use the forces of wind and weather to their advantage.

Sorcerers (caster class) create original magic. Their spells can be a bit raw and out of control, because they are works in progress. They are able to cast spells that can spread damage over a wide area, and can control the actions of their enemies. Sorcerers strive to increase their power.

Healers (caster class) channel magic that keeps friends and group mates healthy during dangerous battles. They can also resurrect group mates once the fight is over.

Rangers (ranged weapons specialist) are more durable than healers and sorcerers, because they wear leather armor. They do a great deal of damage up close, as long as they don't need to stay there. Like casters, however, they're most powerful at a distance. They're excellent with a bow and arrow and throwing knives, and also control an NPC pet that acts as a tank and participates in defense.

COMMON TERMS AND ACRONYMS

Add: an additional monster that joins a battle

Aggro: when a monster focuses on a player in order to attack. A tank always tries to hold a monster's aggro, because if the monster focuses on a more vulnerable class, the character will probably die.

Avatar: character, toon. Your Discordian alter ego

Boss: a monster that is particularly challenging to fight. It's usually three or four levels higher than the stated level.

Caster: abbreviation for spell-caster. This class includes druids, sorcerers, and healers, who use magic to heal, fight, or resurrect dead players when a battle is over.

Combat pet: an NPC animal controlled by a ranger. Used as a tank or a weapon

Cooldown: waiting time before a weapon, ability, or spell can be used again

Critter: a nonaggressive NPC animal

Drop: treasure that a monster leaves behind when it is killed. Loot

Dungeon (aka "dungeon instance" or an "instance"): combat area that is programmed to give each group its own copy of the space, so it doesn't have to compete with other groups. Dungeons usually have various rooms, and high-level monsters (bosses) that drop exceptional loot.

Elite: the most powerful monster in a group of bosses. Difficulty level is ten or more levels above the stated level.

FTW: for the win. An act or ability that is responsible for a victory

Gear: general term for armor, weapons, and protective clothing, such as belts, helms, gauntlets, boots

Group: two to five players who form a temporary alliance to accomplish a quest. Groups communicate with each other by using party chat.

Guild: an organized team of players (minimum of ten) who have banded together for mutual support, raids, and fellowship

Incoming: incoming monsters who intend to attack

Key: an object that will relocate your character to your registered inn

LFG: looking for group

Log: disconnect from the game

Loot: (see "Drop")

Lvl: level

Mob: mobile NPC that is either monster, human, or humanoid. Usually implies hostility

Noob (aka "newb," "newbie," "n00b"): If you're reading this glossary, you.

NPC: nonplayable character. Can be monster, human, or humanoid

Portal: the entrance to a dungeon instance

Primo: a unique, rare, highly coveted piece of gear

PSW: please send whisper

Pull: to lure a single monster from a group without aggroing the others. This strategy allows a group to fight and defeat several mobs at a time. An unsuccessful pull will trigger a mass attack by all the mobs, ending with the inevitable wipeout.

Raid: highly strategic battles involving groups of twenty or more, against elite monsters

Respawn: when a slain monster regenerates

Rez: resurrect. Healers and druids have rez ability, i.e. bring players back to life once a battle is over.

RL: real life. A player's humdrum existence outside Discordia

Soul bound (aka bind on pickup or "bop"): once a player clicks on his loot, it can't be sold to others.

Tank: player or NPC pet whose job it is to hold aggro

Trash: loot with almost no value or utility

Whisper: private conversation between two players that can't be read by the rest of the group

Wipe (aka wipeout): when a party or group of players are all killed by enemies (wiped out)

Vendor: NPC merchant who buys and sells items

CAUTION

Overimmersion in this or in any other online game may lead to an unhealthy dependence or even addiction. If you can no longer remember the last time you saw the sun, WorldsWithoutEnd, Ltd. strongly urges you to get off your butt and go outside.